JOSEPH BRUCHAC

To my teachers,
may I be worthy of them

To my students,
may I be worthy of them

—JB

Text copyright © 2007 by Joseph Bruchac

Cover photo copyright © Getty Images, Chad Baker/Ryan McVay
Design by Shae I. Strunk

Cataloging-in-Publication
Bruchac, Joseph, 1942-
The Way : a novel / by Joseph Bruchac.
        p. ; cm.
ISBN 978-1-58196-062-4
Summary: Cody LeBeau is the new kid at school and the new target for the bullies. He's
Abenaki, like most of the school, but still doesn't fit in. Things begin to change when his
uncle comes to town for a martial arts competition and he and Cody begin training
together.
1. Martial arts—Juvenile fiction. 2. Self-confidence—Juvenile fiction.
3. Abenaki Indians—Juvenile fiction. [1. Martial arts—Fiction.
2. Self-confidence—Fiction. 3. Abenaki Indians—Fiction.] I. Title.
PZ7.B82816 Way 2007
[Fic] dc22
OCLC: 84842708

Published by Darby Creek Publishing
7858 Industrial Parkway
Plain City, OH 43064
www.darbycreekpublishing.com
Printed in the United States

1 2 3 4 5 6 7 8 9

Contents

Acknowledgments

It has been a long time since I was in high school as a student. I could not have written this book without the assistance of those young men and women who helped me understand a little of what life is like as an American high school student in the 21st century.

Special thanks, in particular, to the Saratoga Springs High School students in Mark Oppenneer's classes who answered so many of my questions with such detail, intelligence, and good humor.

Chapter 1

NINJA DREAMS

The traveler passes.
The road remains.
—Sensei Ni

No one even notices me. No one ever notices a ninja until it is too late. Those terrorists don't realize whose school they are messing with. They haven't reckoned with Cody LeBeau, who has long been secretly studying every mysterious form of deadly unarmed combat. Just when those bad guys are about to start bumping off kids, I scream like an angry eagle and come flying in *a la* Bruce Lee in *Return of the Dragon* or Tony Laa in *Ong Bak, Thai Warrior*. It's happening so fast that even *I* don't know exactly what's happening—except that *I* am knocking the guns out of their hands and subduing them one after another. Soon every single terrorist is lying at my feet, and everyone is staring at me in wonder. Even Maya.

Maya is this girl with long dark hair who I have sort of noticed from time to time. She's in my English class. I've seen her reading poetry, but she's not an Emo. You know the ones I mean. Those emotional kids who listen to the most dramatic, depressing music and wear their hair so it hangs down over their faces as they walk around sort of weeping over the unfairness of the world. Kind of the opposites of the preppy girls and the chirpy cheerleader chicks.

Maya doesn't seem to fit into any one clique, though. She's pretty much friendly with everyone in a non-gushy way. She's even nodded to me now and then. I kind of like the way she pushes back her hair with one hand while she's reading and does this little pouty thing with her lips that shows she is really thinking hard about the words on the page.

Anyway, getting back to my fantasy. Maya is staring at me. Looking up at me, her dark eyes wide.

"Oh Cody!" she says, touching my arm. "I never knew that you were so incredible." Then she gasps. "You're bleeding!"

I reach up to touch my chest. My warm lifeblood is flowing in a crimson stream down my perfectly tailored white shirt that has come open at the top to expose my bulging pectoral muscles, built up from all those days of secret training developing the iron-palm technique that has failed to protect me from the armor-piercing bullet fired from the last evildoer's gun just before I knocked him out with a perfectly executed backfist. (I don't have a white shirt now, but since I have one in my fantasy, I am clearly destined to own one. I'm not so sure about those pecs, though.)

"It is nothing," I reply with a regretful but manly smile. "All it hit was my heart. I am just glad I was able to save everyone."

Then everything goes black. But only for a moment, because then I am at my funeral. Everyone is there, everyone I ever knew. The kids are all wearing black armbands, crying and carrying signs that read:

CODY, OUR HERO

WE MISS YOU, CODY

and

YOU WERE THE GREATEST

"I tripped him in the lunchroom," Brett says in a choked voice, "but he gave his life for me. He was the finest man I ever knew."

"I will always love him and never forget him," Maya says between sobs.

The principal is holding up a plaque. Everyone goes silent.

"He saved us all," Mr. Ross rumbles, his voice filled with deep emotion. "So, in his honor, we are renaming our school." Then he reads the words: "CODY LeBEAU HIGH," and everyone cheers—briefly—before they go back to sobbing again.

Mom and Dad are there, of course. They are holding hands and weeping over my grave. My martyr's death has brought them back together.

"I am so proud of him," Mom says.

"Yes," my father agrees. "I am proud, too." He pauses and shakes his head. "Even though he was such a screw-up and a loser."

Screw-up? Loser? What are those words doing in my fantasy? Why, in fact, am I hearing them out loud?

"Hey, screw-up! Wake up, loser," a sarcastic voice yells.

I open my eyes. The bus is in front of me, the door open. Mike, the driver, exasperatedly beckons to me with one hand while Grey Cook—the tall, skinny Koacook kid on my bus who has already, after only my first two weeks of school, pegged me as the easiest and almost daily target for his verbal abuse—is leaning out a window. He's making another hand gesture in my direction that is even more pointed than Mike's weary wave.

"Yo, loser," Grey hoots, "nappy-nap's over. Climb on duh bus."

Fists of impotent fury clenched at my side, I climb on, but not without stumbling on the second step and scraping my knee.

Yet another glorious, new day.

Chapter 2

NO ONE SITS WITH ME

Expect nothing.
Rejoice when you get it.
—Sifu Sahn

The one good thing about the ride to school is that I can have a little privacy. No one ever sits with me on the bus. It's a new bus with lots of room in it. All the buses in the district are new because of the casino. It has pumped so much money into the community as a whole—not just the Koacook Tribe—that they don't have to make do with a fleet of aging and overcrowded yellow clunkers like the perennially backfiring rusty cattle cars they called buses back at my last school. They only had a dozen buses for the whole junior high, and they packed them like cattle cars, chugging from one trailer park to the next. I had to get up an hour and a half before school because the bus ride was so long.

That wasn't as hard for me as it was for some kids. Mom always got me up early. "My grampa told me you have to greet the new day along with the first songs of the birds," she would say back then. But these days she finds herself going to bed just as I am getting up. The newest hires at the casino get stuck with the graveyard shifts and the hours no one else wants. This week hers are from 8 P.M. until 5 A.M.

"My morning bird songs are now lullabies," she said this morning.

I smiled back at her, as if it really was a funny joke and not another example of how upside-down our lives have become since Dad decided to make *his* life as an over-the-road trucker separate from ours.

A year before we moved here, Dad started looking off into the distance whenever he was home. He and Mom stopped making eye contact. I read their body language like it was an open book. Even though I wanted to scream when he said it, it didn't surprise me when he said he'd signed on for more long-haul assignments. Trucking lettuce from the San Fernando Valley to Boston. Turning around for another four-day run and not ever coming home. Not when Mom and me were living up near Green Bay. Not even down here to the Koacook Rez—even though we're just an hour's drive from Beantown.

It doesn't feel much like a family now that it's just Mom and me. The only relatives I know now are from Mom's stories about them.

I wish I'd known Mom's grampa. Just from the stories she's told me that he passed on to her, he must have been really cool. But he died of diabetes way before I was born. So did my grandparents on both sides of my family. Well, not exactly. Actually only one of them died of diabetes, and one of my grandmothers lived to see me as a toddler. Grandfather LeBeau was taken by cancer, and Grandmother LeBeau died in a car accident. Mom's dad, Grampa Wadzo, was, we assume, a casualty of that long-ago war that was fought in Vietnam.

Did you notice that I said that we *assumed* Grandfather Wadzo died in Vietnam? He went MIA during the withdrawal of American troops in 1972 and was never found. Mom was born three months after he disappeared, and Grama Wadzo was only eighteen years old. She'd married him while he was home on leave. She must have loved him, though, because she just kept waiting for him to return, and she never got married again.

Grama Wadzo was the only one of my ill-fated grandparents that I ever met. I am pretty sure I remember her holding me when I was two years old. Grama Christine. A warm, round face smiling down at me. She lived just long enough to get snuffed out by a heart attack at the ripe old age of forty. Nowadays nobody seems destined to survive past the age of forty on either side of my family.

Mom says that back in the old days, before people ate all this sugar and white bread, when we lived off the land, our people lived a very long time. To live for over a hundred winters was no big deal. Some of them were like those Taoist monks in China who lived so long they were called Immortals. Like Pai Mei in *Kill Bill*. Brown rice and green tea and exercise and deep breathing. That was their secret for living two or even three hundred years. None of that candy and junk food and soda pop in their diet. Like the stuff that they sell in the vending machines just outside the cafeteria at Long River High.

Memo to self: *Add brown rice to grocery list.* I think they have that, at least, in the Price Giant. (As soon as Mom has the car paid off and she's gotten ahead on the rent for the trailer, she says she plans on budgeting extra money so we can get some of the items I've been lecturing her about from the one health food store in town. But for now I can make a first step toward immortality with brown rice. And get Mom on that diet, too. She's almost thirty-five, which means she is getting perilously close to the point where she'll be living on borrowed time.)

I usually do the grocery shopping since Mom is so tired

after those long nights waitressing and serving drinks to semi-catatonic retirees who are wearing out their rotator cuff muscles in their right shoulders by pulling the lever on the slot machine they've chosen to feed for six hours straight. The theory, Mom says, is that as soon as you stop feeding a machine, it'll pay off for someone else. Some of those folks—and not the oldest ones either—actually wear adult diapers while they're playing so they don't have to get up and go to the bathroom.

The bus's wheels thud over something in the road. I hope it's just a piece of tire and not something that was alive. I stare out the window. Nothing much to see yet. The sun hasn't come up over the hills. But I might catch a glimpse of a deer's eyes reflecting the lights from the bus. There's a lot of deer around the reservation. I read in the *Koacook Courier* that they're eating up all the imported ornamentals that some people have planted as hedges around the neatly mowed yards that surround their big, new houses. There are no natural predators like wolves and mountain lions any more. The tribal council has been trying to get more Koacook tribal members to do bow hunting to cut down the numbers. But no one here is interested. Why hunt deer when you have enough money to buy porterhouse every night? A lot of deer, though, get hit by cars. So I am always thinking about them as we roar along the newly paved road through the predawn hour. I'm sending them mental messages to stay back and not step out to get whacked.

Over the squawk and thud of different tunes leaking out of too-loud iPods plugged into ears headed down the road to early deafness, I can hear someone snoring behind me. I can sympathize. Why do the powers that be in this world insist that high school students have to go to school earlier than the younger kids? I just scanned an article in a science magazine about a study that proves that teenagers need to sleep later. That is why so many of us are half-asleep for the first three periods every day. Our biorhythms are just different.

Tell that to the school board. Or to the football coaches who want to make sure the day is done early enough to get their boys out onto the practice field.

I am going into my mental rant about education again and how messed up it is. From start to finish. It is even worse if you are Indian, because one of the first things they do is tell you that the only thing real in the world is science and all your traditional beliefs are just superstition. And what is the result of science? A world full of people fighting each other and destroying the environment.

In the old days people learned from the natural world. Everything made sense and it all worked together. The old stories were about things like how the earth itself was shaped on the back of a turtle from the mud that the diving birds and animals brought up from the bottom. They taught lessons that really helped us. Like showing us how cooperation makes great things possible.

Tell that to my earth science teacher. Like I did last week. He was not amused by my superstitious take on continent building.

"That's enough fairy stories, LeBeau," he said halfway through my recitation of our old story of how the world was created.

"But I'm not done yet!" I said, refusing to sit down.

"Oh, yes, you are," he growled.

Yup, that was the most recent incident in which my big mouth ended up getting me sent to the principal's office.

I breathe on the window. It is just cold enough outside for my breath to make a cloud of mist. I draw a circle in it with my index finger. I want to go back to the circle. That is the secret in karate and aikido and all the other arts. The circle. Move in a circle, and you repel all your attackers. You turn their force back against them.

I think about moving my feet the way I saw an aikido master do it in a TV show. Your two feet make kind of like a *T* shape. I look down at my feet and groan. I've done it again. I was half-asleep when I got dressed and I put on the wrong sneakers, the old comfortable ones that are the wrong brand. Nobody at school wears shoes like these.

They all wear the newest expensive designer brands with the names of basketball players on them. Not only that, my feet are so big that everybody will really notice. I'm only 5'4", but I take a size eleven. All day I'm going to be hearing such charmingly clever comments as:

Look, he's got his clown shoes on.

Hey, kid, I gotta take a trip. Can I borrow one of your canoes?

I'd be better off if I just heaved them out the window and went barefoot.

Chapter 3

JUST ANOTHER DAY

A good explanation

explains nothing.

—Master Net

It's turned out to be just another day. Surprisingly, I managed to avoid drawing attention to my shoes. For the first half hour of the day.

It started off well enough. I made sure I was the last one to get off the bus. I didn't even react when Grey Cook slapped me in the back of my head as he passed my seat. I just pretended I didn't notice because I was so busy fixing a strap on my old non-designer-label backpack. I did, however, imagine what the scenario would have been had I disclosed my mastery of the ancient arts. (Remember, dear reader, that in my imagination I am the master of them all.) In this case, Northern Shaolin kung fu wu su.

In my imaginary scene, Grey's slap never lands. Instead,

as if I have eyes in the back of my head (the byproduct of countless hours of training), I lift my right arm and block his slap, which in my imagination is no longer just a lazy open hand, but is now a vicious, killing blow aimed at the back of my neck. Not only that, Grey is no longer a skinny kid—he has been transformed into a hugely muscled attacker wearing a black mask who's not trying to hit me with his hand, but with a club. He's about to hijack the school bus and hold all the Indian kids hostage until the casino pays him a ten-million-dollar ransom. (Chump change for them, I might add. The Koacook casino is—in real life and not just my fantasy world—the fourth most profitable Indian casino in North America.)

Grey Black-Mask knows, though, that he has to take me out first. Otherwise, I may thwart his evil scheme. Since I saved our school from those terrorists, my reputation has spread. He swings at me with his other hand—the one that is holding an iron bar, but I block it just as easily with my same hand, my block so precisely aimed at the nerve center in his wrist that it paralyzes his hand, and the iron bar falls clanking onto the floor of the bus. Then, with great precision, my hand a blur of movement too fast for the ordinary human eye to see, I strike him square in the center of his chest with an iron-palm technique. It hurls him backward through the front window of the bus, which explodes into a shower of glass.

I'm about to turn around, both to see if there are any other hijackers for me to dispose of and also to accept, modestly, of course, the accolades of the other kids on the bus for saving their lives, even though they didn't deserve it.

However, I was interrupted by a weary voice.

"Come on, LeBeau, you're not hurt. Stop rubbing your head and get off the bus. I've got to get back to the garage."

It was Mike the bus driver. I opened my eyes and got up.

Mike stopped me with one hand on my shoulder. "Don't worry. I got my eyes on him. I won't let him get at you on my bus again, okay?"

I nodded. It would have been better, though, if Mike hadn't been kind. Better still if he hadn't even seen me getting whacked.

"Want me to say something about it to the A.P.?" Mike asked.

I shook my head and turned away from him to wipe the moisture out of my eyes. It had to be allergies because here's no way I'd have cried just because I got swatted like I was some insignificant little gnat. Then I slipped past Mike and down the stairs.

I wasn't really rubbing the back of my head where Grey slapped me because it hurt. It had just surprised me and then started me thinking about what I might have done if things had been different. It didn't hurt even one little . . . Okay, I'll be honest. It *did* hurt, but only because it was embarrassing. Not physically. It's hard to hurt me physically, even if the other kids don't know that. I may be little, but all of my years of climbing trees—and sometimes falling out of them—have toughened me up physically. Even when I get bruises, they go away almost overnight.

Like this one time when I was trying to build a treehouse in an old apple tree in an abandoned orchard across from where Mom and I lived 3TPA (three trailer parks ago). I was in seventh grade then. There was also a broken-roofed shed buried in the weeds of that orchard, and I was going to use the rusty tools and old boards I'd found in it. But first I had to cut some branches out of the way.

The first big branch was hung up in the branches above it. When I cut through, the butt of that branch thudded back against me so hard that I went flying out of the tree and landed on my back twenty feet below. I lay there, still holding the saw in my right hand and staring up at the sky and not being able to breathe for what felt like forever. Or at least long enough to wonder if I was dead and about to go up into those white clouds floating above me. Then my breath finally came back into me, and I felt even worse. *I'm an idiot*, I thought. *I can't do anything right.*

I put that saw and the other tools back into the shed and

limped home. I was covered with bruises the next day, but two days later, I never would have known—aside from the addition of another embarrassing memory—I'd been beat up by a fruit tree.

Things went okay for a while after getting off the bus. I managed to get into class without talking to anyone, tucked my feet under me so they wouldn't be noticed, and put my head down. I succeeded in keeping a super-low profile until Ms. Taker reached my name at roll call, which is always taken during first period, her English class.

"Mr. Leee-booo?" she said, drawing out my name, dramatically as usual.

Don't ask me why she does that. Maybe she is trying to be funny. Ms. Taker is in her second year of teaching high school and doesn't look much older than the kids in her classes. My guess is that she's unsure of herself. I've noticed the way she constantly clasps and unclasps her hands when she talks to us. She makes some of the girls giggle when she says their names that way—like they are sharing some secret joke together. I hate it, though. But this time I didn't try to correct her.

"Here." That is all I said, not too loud, so it wouldn't draw attention to me.

Unfortunately, I said it too softly.

"Cody," Ms. Taker said, looking down at me over the

21

roll sheet, "you have such a beautiful voice. Why don't you use it and speak up so we can all hear you?"

A beautiful voice. I knew that everyone in the class heard her. Before she takes the roll, Ms. Taker always orders her students to unplug and close up their cell phones. That way she gets their undivided, though bored, attention. I groaned inside at her thoughtless remark, which I was now destined to hear thrown back at me in various forms for the rest of the day. I couldn't even think of a single kung fu fantasy that would turn it around.

I knew what was going to happen. Teenagers are like most other pack animals when they sense weakness. Word would spread about my having a "beautiful voice," and I'd be teased everywhere I went. When it comes to teasing, I've discovered from the various schools I have attended, Indian kids can be even worse than white kids. And not just to outsiders like me.

My mind flashed back to what had happened to Stump during my third day here. Stump is a kid in my class—his real name is Jackson Teeter. He's Koacook and his father is the head of security at the casino. But Jackson is so grungy—it's not just the acne, but that brown flak jacket and the black jeans and sneakers he always wears—that he doesn't have any friends. He's not small like me. He's about six feet tall, but he's no athlete. His arms are skinny, and the rest of his body is fat.

I may be little, but at least I'm not strange-looking. I'm just average. The features in my brown-skinned face aren't anything special, nothing to make any girl take notice. My hair is jet black, like my eyes, but I keep my hair short and a little spiky. I don't wear it shoulder-length to emphasize the fact that I'm a Skin like some of the Koacook guys. There's nothing different or special about me at all.

Stump, though, stands out in any crowd. He gets picked on almost automatically, like he's asking for it. Not that anyone deliberately makes an attempt to bully him. More like if he strays a little too close to anyone in the hall, they give him a shove and say something mean like, "Back off, loser!" Kind of like swatting at a fly.

On that third day in this school, I was in the library when I heard some really loud laughter from the hall just outside. Through the display window I could see a group of big guys—junior and senior football players. I didn't go out there. Being a freshman, a low bird in the pecking order, I knew enough to keep out of the way of those upper-class boys.

Probably one of them's making dumb jokes about sex. That's what I thought at first. Then, as I stretched up on my toes to peer around *Touching Spirit Bear*, *The Buffalo Tree*, and the other books in display in the window, I saw what they were all howling like hyenas about. Somebody had pantsed Stump. He was sitting on the floor with his back against the wall, his jeans down around his ankles, and his skinny knees showing. A broad-shouldered Koacook kid stood over Stump. It was Brett Sonaqua, the senior captain of the school's undefeated football team, leader of that gang of guys who command the head table in the lunchroom and stick out their legs so little kids who try to get past them trip and spill their lunch trays all over themselves and then end up having to spend the whole day smelling like soured milk.

Brett was pointing something at Stump. It was one of those hyper-tech new phones that can record a short video.

"Stumpie-dumpie," Brett said, laughing, "smile for the camera. You are going to be a star on YouTube."

"Clear the hall!" a harsh voice rumbled.

The crowd evaporated as Mr. Mennis, the assistant principal, lumbered around the corner.

By the time the A.P. got to him, Stump had already picked himself up off the floor and pulled up his pants. His face was expressionless. He already had his notebook and his black pen in his hands.

That's another strange thing about Stump. Whatever happens to him, he never complains or fights back. He just takes out that little brown notebook he keeps in an inside pocket and scribbles in it. Weird.

Thinking back on what happened to Stump, I knew I

couldn't just stand there and take it the way he did. I could only hold my tongue just so long before I'd crack and say something smartass with my big mouth. And then things would just get worse.

Maybe, I thought, *maybe I was wrong. Maybe nobody really noticed what Ms. Taker said.*

But I wasn't wrong. Just as I'd feared, the teasing started right after the bell to change classes. As I walked down the hall trying to be invisible, the mocking voices started up from behind me.

"Hey, Lee-booo, why don't you sing something with that beautiful voice of yours?"

"Hey, Pretty Voice!"

"Little Bitty Pretty Voice!"

"Why aren't you singing?"

"Cuz he's a baby. Babies don't sing, they cry."

"What's wrong, baby? Did you wet your pants?"

And then I cracked.

So here I am, sitting in the nurse's office holding a Kleenex up to my nose and pinching my nostrils together. There's a wad of bloody tissues on the bench next to me. I'm pretty sure the bleeding has stopped now, but the nurse told me not to stop squeezing until she comes back.

I'm in no hurry for that. I know that the next stop after the nurse turns me loose will be the A.P.'s office.

"Mr. LeBeau," Mr. Mennis rasps, steepling his fingers together and rocking back on his chair as he stares at me from behind his desk. "Why are you always fighting?"

I look down at the floor. It probably pleases him that I do that. My body language is telling him that I know he's in control and that I'm feeling regretful. Just like his body language—holding his hands up with the fingertips touching, sitting back in his padded chair while I'm on this uncomfortable wooden stool—is a sure sign of his self-satisfied superiority. He probably doesn't even know he's doing that. And I am not about to tell him. I'm dumb, but not that stupid.

"I wasn't fighting," I say in a low voice.

The A.P. sits forward suddenly, letting the front legs of his chair hit the floor with a loud crack. "What?" he snaps, slapping his hands on the desk.

I jump, but only because I know I'm supposed to. I've been here before, and I have his entire act memorized, including the part I'm supposed to play. After eight different schools, in six years, I have pretty much figured out what it takes to be an assistant principal. Intimidation is a major ingredient in the recipe.

I look up at him and then speak a little louder. "I wasn't fighting, sir," I say.

The "sir" pleases him, but he tries not to show that.

"Then how did you get *that*?" Mr. Mennis asks, pointing

at my swollen nose. He sits back in his chair, certain that he has just shown the winning card. But he doesn't know what I have in my hand. Nothing.

"Punching bags don't get into fights," I mumble.

"What?" he says. He's not sure he's heard me right.

"Getting hit by somebody's backpack," I reply. "Accidentally, I mean—that's not getting into a fight."

The A.P. narrows his eyes. "Are you saying that this was an accident, that you just happened to get hit in the face by someone's backpack?"

Well, that isn't exactly what I said. But I'm not lying to him when I answer, "The halls are really crowded. It's easy for somebody to bump into another person without even knowing it, especially if he's late for the next period."

Mr. Mennis steeples his hands again. He's thinking. I am pretty sure I can read his mind. There's a no-tolerance policy at Long River High for fighting—an automatic suspension for all parties involved. Even the kid who gets his butt kicked is kicked out for two days. If Mr. Mennis takes this further and I get suspended along with whomever may have hit me—a party whose identity shall remain unknown to the A.P., for I may be a big mouth but I will never be a narc—it becomes an official "incident," and he'll have to write a detailed report.

However, if it was just a minor accident, no injury

intended, then there's no need for more paperwork on his part. And it does not become part of the record, a record that is scrutinized by the school board—a school board that praises the school administrators when the number of violent incidents stays low or goes down.

I see him reach his decision by the way he looks off to the side for a moment. I may not have lied, but he has decided to be satisfied with what he is certain has to be deception. He nods and then stands up to loom over me, which is not hard for him to do, since he was a college basketball player before becoming a P.E. instructor and then an A.P. He's got at least a foot and a half on me!

"You can go, LeBeau. But remember," Mr. Mennis thumps his huge hand against his chest and then raises his index finger ominously, "I've got my eyes on you."

As I exit his office, I catch a glimpse of Jeff Chahna. He's back in the hallway, out of sight of the A.P.'s door. He's looking worried because a suspension will mean he won't be able to play in the football game tomorrow. He's one of Brett Sonaqua's gang of jocks, the starting halfback on our team, which is eighty percent made up of Indian kids, and we're playing our biggest rival this weekend. Jeff's eyes meet mine. Koacook warrior sees an Abenaki stranger in the forest. Is he an enemy or a friend? Neither, I think.

I don't say anything. I just lift my right hand and swing

it off to the side, palm down as I shake my head. He gets it. I didn't squeal that it was his fist that hit my face after I spun around and told him, "Your lack of intellect is a perfect match for your Neanderthal physiognomy." I'd even lifted my chin and shoved my face at him.

Don't ask me why I did that. I knew that even if he didn't understand what I'd said, the tone of my voice and my stance made it clear that I was challenging him. I knew he'd probably throw a punch at me. And I knew I wouldn't be able to duck it.

I was right on all three counts. Predicting future personal disasters is one of my specialties. But not squealing.

I see the relief in Jeff Chahna's eyes. Then the bell rings. The hall fills with kids, and I lose sight of him.

I sigh. Time to head off to my next class. Earth science. Oh joy! But as I turn, I catch sight of someone else further down the hall—a big, sloppy shape in a flak jacket leaning back into his locker. As usual, he's got that little brown notebook out, and he's writing in it.

Just another day.

Chapter 4

A STRANGER COMES TO TOWN

Eyes closed,
the real reading begins.
—Pendetta Satu

The one good thing about every day at school—aside from the end of every day at school—is that I can usually find time to get into the library. It's the only place I feel at home, even if it is woefully lacking in books about the Asian fighting arts. For some reason, the school encourages football—where two-hundred-pound lunks hit each other with their whole bodies, routinely breaking limbs and giving each other concussions—but the administration has a positively paranoid fear of anything that has to do with punching and kicking. Thus, no books about kung fu, aikido, tae kwan do, karate, even boxing and judo! Or so they think.

But there is a selection of books about the Far East,

including Japan, China and Korea, and in each of them I've found at least a few paragraphs about my favorite topics. Our librarian, Mrs. Masters, is well aware of my real interest and has a habit of searching out books she knows I'll enjoy. I know she's also hoping I'll outgrow my fascination with martial mayhem. So she includes books of translated Chinese and Japanese poetry in the stuff she unearths or gets through interlibrary loan that make mention of fighting techniques. She also uses her home computer to download and print out articles that are directly about you-know-what.

I don't have a computer at home, which makes me the only kid in the universe without Internet access. The only computers I ever get to use are at school where they have plenty of blocking software to keep us from getting off-task and into anything really interesting during the few hours a day we get access. Mom keeps promising that as soon as she is able to set enough money aside, she'll get us a computer and DSL. For now, just paying the electricity and water and phone bills every month is all she can afford in the way of luxuries. (Joke.) We don't even have cable on our pathetic thirteen-inch television.

Anyhow, back to Mrs. Masters. She folds up the articles that she prints out and tucks them—a single page at a time—into such books as Arthur Waley's *The Poetry and Career of Li Po.* She'd probably get into big trouble for doing it if the powers-that-be knew. Of course, I realize her strategy is meant to encourage me to turn page after page of those collections of haikus and tankas from ancient Japan, to search through the Tang Dynasty verses of Tu Fu and Li Po in search of the newest page on Shotokan karate that gives a bio of Master Gichin Funakoshi, the style's great and honorable founder. She knows the kind of reader I am—if I see words on a page, they catch me the way a fly gets stuck in the web of a spider. Then I have to read them before I can get free.

As a result of Mrs. Masters, Li Po has become my favorite writer these days. He wasn't just a poet, but also a famous swordsman. When he was a young man, he traveled around Szechuan Province as a *hsieh*, a kind of wandering knight who took it upon himself to avenge wrongs done against those who had no way to defend themselves, especially women and children. As Wei Hao, his best friend, put it, "Mr. Li ran his sword through quite a number of people." Cool.

But he also went and lived in the mountains far from any human beings, where rare birds ate from his hands. There are times I wish I could do that, just get away from everything in the modern world and be like my ancestors, connected to everything. Here's one of Li Po's poems about that:

Ask me why I dwell among green mountains,
I laugh silently; my soul is serene.
Peach blossom follows moving water.
Another heaven and earth exist beyond the world of men.

Anyhow, getting back to my time in the library, which is where I am spending the last half hour of this disastrous day, keeping my swollen nose, my blood-stained shirt, my ugly backpack, and my Bozo sneakers out of sight of all prying eyes by sitting slouched in a beanbag chair half under the furthest back table behind the bookshelves, I feel the presence of someone nearby and look up from my reading of *The White Pony, an Anthology of Chinese Poetry* to see that I am, indeed, not alone. (Bet you thought I was never going to finish that sentence.) It's Mrs. Masters. She's holding out a box of tissues. I grab one just in time to catch the glob of blood that was about to plop from my snout onto the page.

She doesn't say anything, which is kind of unusual. Mrs. Masters talks more than most of my teachers. Contrary to popular belief, librarians are *not* the silent type. Having been to more schools than most, I consider myself an expert on the topic. Librarians are always talking about the books that excite them and trying to hook reluctant students into reading by reading aloud to them. But not today. Mrs. Masters is just looking at me. I finally crack first.

"What?" I say. It comes out hostile, different than I mean it.

"You're a good kid, Cody," she says, ignoring my crabbiness. "Give yourself a break, okay?"

Mrs. Masters taps her index finger on the table. It's a sort of nervous habit that she does when she is thinking. Nobody reads body language like me. Like when she runs her fingers through her tightly curled, short, blond hair and tosses her head back, I know that what she is reading behind her desk isn't school-related. It's one of those women's magazines she sneaks in. *Cosmopolitan*, usually. She hides it in the same drawer with her stash of dark chocolate.

Tapping her finger that way, though, means she's just found some pearl of wisdom to bestow upon an unsuspecting teenager, usually as a result of something she's just read. She taps her finger and nods, then closes whatever book or magazine she has in her hands.

"Every story," she says, "always seems to start one of two ways." She holds up the thumb on her right hand. "Someone goes on a journey."

I nod again. That's been the sum total of my life story so far. Someone goes on a journey and then another and then another and then . . .

Mrs. Masters taps on the table again. Not her "I'm thinking" tap. This is her "pay attention" one. Then she holds up the thumb on her left hand. "Or a stranger comes to town and changes everything."

I don't nod this time. I don't quite get it.

I wait for the punch line, but that's it. Mrs. Masters gets up, message delivered, and goes back to her desk. Two minutes later the bell rings. I wait till the hall is clear, and then I slink out to my bus, wishing I had a ninja master's ability to cloak himself in invisibility.

The bus trip home is uneventful this time. Grey—the jerk—isn't on board, for one. Probably attending some after-school club. His father will pick him up in his huge new Humvee that gets about two miles to the gallon. He'll take him out for ice cream on their way home. I've seen them cruise by, Grey looking all superior, and his father behind the wheel in control of the universe.

I hate them both.

That thought startles me. When did I start hating people I don't really know?

I trudge up the short walkway to the door of the trailer. It swings open before I can get there. My mom's not only awake, she's beaming at me from the doorway. She has on a new blouse, and she is positively glowing.

"Cody," she says in a happier voice than I've heard since I don't know when. "Your uncle is here!"

Chapter 5

WHAT UNCLE?

One cannot fill
a cup held upside down.
—Sensei Ni

"Your uncle is here."

"What uncle?"

That is what I'm thinking. But Mom's words have surprised me so much that I don't just think that question—I say it out loud. Not only that, but my tone is suspicious, defensive, and sarcastic. It's the tone of voice that has become Cody LeBeau's typical verbal response to the increasingly mean and disappointing world around him.

Great, I think. *I've become the stereotypical sullen teenager of a B-movie.*

Of course, knowing that doesn't stop me from still acting the part. Neither does the hurt look that is starting to show on Mom's face.

This is the first time I've hit her with this side of me. Until now I've kept my bitter waves of emotion closed behind such meaningless responses as "I'm fine" or "Everything's cool" or the all-purpose "Okay" whenever she's asked me how I am and how things are going.

Mom recomposes her face. "Your Uncle John," she says.

"I don't have an Uncle John," I snap back.

Oh wonderful! I'm not just letting loose a wave of hostility. It's turning into a tsunami.

Still, I'm sure I don't have an uncle named John. Since my dad's younger brother Louis got blown up in Iraq three years ago, I don't have any uncles left. I know that in the old days, our people had extended families nearby in the village or even in the same wigwam. Grandparents, brother and sisters, lots of cousins and uncles and aunts. But this is the twenty-first century, and the only place you find families like that now is among Indians still living on their own rez.

Kids who are lucky have at best a mother and a father and maybe one or two siblings. But I'm not lucky. I'm a modern, semi-orphan, Indian nomad from a sort-of-broken home. If you can call a rundown, five-room trailer a home.

Mom closes the door behind her and sits down on the steps. She holds out her hand to me, and even though this angry, stubborn part of me that seems to have taken control fights it, I find myself reaching out and grasping her fingers. Conditioned reflex. Some of the tension lets go of me, and I sit down next to her.

She looks close at me and notices my swollen nose and the blood dried under my left nostril. She was so excited that she hadn't even noticed till now.

"What happened to you?" she asks, soft concern and worry mixed in equal parts into her voice.

"Nothing much. I just ran into something hard."

All true. My getting punched is nothing much. Par for the course for Cody LeBeau. And Jeff Chahna's big, bony fist was, for sure, something hard.

Usually Mom would not let it go at that. She'd keep grilling me. But not today.

"Cody," she says, "I never told you about your Uncle John, my little brother, before because it's . . . a complicated story."

"A brother?" I ask. Mom's hesitant way of saying it has convinced me I am ready to hear her story.

"After your Grampa Matthew disappeared, Grama Christine waited for him. She never got married again."

"I know that." I can't help interrupting. Part of me wants to jump up and run away. But Mom tightens her grip on my shoulder. Even Dad, who was a tough trucker, was never able to break her grip when she took hold of him. Strong hands run in her side of the family. Mom and Dad used to joke about it—until she just stopped holding on to him.

"Listen," she says. "Grama Christine . . . my mother—" Mom stops. She's tugging at her hair with the hand that isn't holding me, and she's biting her lip. What she has to say is hard for her. I can sense that this is the point where I could interrupt, shut her up with a wise-ass remark, keep her from spilling a family secret that I never suspected. But instead I am holding my breath.

"Cody," Mom whispers, "four years after my father went missing, my mother had another child."

"How could she have another child if her husband wasn't around?" I realize it is the world's dumbest question, so stupid that even a ten-year-old wouldn't ask it. But I just blurted it out. I can feel my ears getting red.

Fortunately, Mom lets my embarrassment go unnoticed. "She was lonely," she replies.

"Oh," I say.

Mom sighs. She's gotten it out now.

"She . . . met another man. She never even told me the man's name. From what little Mother did tell me, he was Indian, too, but he was just traveling through, and she never saw him again. The result was my brother, my half-brother. Your Uncle John.

"Everyone knew about it, of course. Even though Mom didn't keep the baby. She was still hoping that Grampa Matthew might return—and how could she explain this child to him? One of her best friends who lived out in the Midwest and didn't have children of her own took John in. She and her husband raised him and gave him their last name." She pauses. "Awassos. John Awassos. So he stayed a bear." She forces a smile and tugs even harder at her hair.

"Oh," I say, trying to smile, but not really succeeding. It's a weak attempt at humor on her part. Our family is bear clan. *Awassos*, the last name of my supposed new uncle, means "bear" in our language.

"My half-brother was the family secret." Mom lets go of that lock of hair before she tugs it out by the roots. "And like most family secrets, everybody knew it and talked about it behind our backs—and then pretended they didn't know about it to our faces. That's why Mother finally told me. I heard people whispering about it when I was thirteen, and I asked her about it. And she told me the truth."

Mom squeezes my shoulder even harder. "I never told you about it because it all seemed so . . . complicated. Especially with everything else happening in our lives." She waves her hand to the side, her gesture taking in the pathetic trailer park, the hostile territory of Koacook, our aimless wandering from place to place, everything we've lost, and everything I know I'll never have. "I thought I'd wait till you were older. I know that doesn't make any sense. Does it?"

I shake my head.

We sit there in silence for a while. Part of me wants to comfort my mom, and part of me feels like it's being sucked into a whirlpool. But there's a question I have to ask.

"Why is . . . ?" It's hard to say the words because they stick in my mouth like glue, but I manage to spit them out. "Why is *my uncle* here now?"

Mom takes another breath. "He and I have been writing letters to each other for a few years now. He started writing them as soon as his adopted mother finally told him about me. When you and I lived in Chicago, I even met him and we had coffee together." Her voice is getting happier again. "It turned out that we were alike in so many ways, Cody. And just knowing I had a brother I could talk with . . . it was . . . it was great. It was like finding another part of myself, a part that was living an exciting life. But because he was in the Marines, he was only home for a short time. He'd been a Marine since he was eighteen."

Mom looks over her shoulder toward our trailer door and the person who is apparently waiting on the other side of it. "I should have told you about John," she says, turning back at me. "But I guess I was being selfish. It was as if he was a hidden part of my life that I couldn't share without losing it. I know that's strange. But his letters were so interesting. They kept me from going crazy."

I look at this unfamiliar woman sitting next to me. Is

this really my mother?

"If you want to read some of his letters," she says, "I can let you see some. The ones he wrote me from Kuwait and Afghanistan and Iraq are amazing. Even after he was wounded, he still kept writing."

Mom thinks she is explaining everything to me, but I'm just feeling more confused. I have to interrupt again. "So why is he here now?"

Mom stands up. "He's been waiting inside until I told you about him," she says. "Why don't we just let him tell you why he's here?"

Chapter 6

SHAKING HANDS

Open hand.
Where does the fist go?
—Sifu Sahn

The tall, broad-shouldered man standing at the far end of the cramped space we laughingly call our living room makes our trailer seem even smaller.

"John," my mother says, her voice sounding happy again, "this is the nephew I've been telling you so much about."

I cringe inwardly at those words. Whenever you get introduced that way, your first thought is that whatever has been told about you is probably wrong. Then your second thought, which makes you cringe even more, is that whatever has been told about you really has described your weak, pathetic, self-pitying self. If I weren't being pushed ahead by my mother, I'd bolt out the door, climb a tree, and live out the rest of my life with the squirrels. Except I would probably be lousy at that, too. All the other squirrels would make jokes

43

about the clumsy new guy with no tail who keeps falling off limbs and can't crack nuts with his teeth worth a darn.

But before I get too lost in my fantasy of a tree-dwelling life, the stranger in my living room turns around in an easy, graceful motion that is surprising for someone that big. He smiles at me. It's not a broad smile, one that shows all his teeth like a phony politician, but there's real warmth in it. Not only that, his smile is accompanied by a familiar little nod. It is exactly the way my mother nods when her smile is for someone she is truly happy to see. In fact, the lean face of John Awassos is so much like my mom's, especially in his eyes and the set of his jaw, that my heart tells me for sure that he really is her brother.

He holds out a hand. "Cody," he says.

Just that. Just my name. But it's the way he says it, in a voice that is about a mile deeper than mine (which lately sounds like a rusty gate being forced open). It's as if he enjoys the sound of my name, as if he is telling me something about my name I've never known before. Like that my name is cool. It makes me wish I could record the way he says my name so if I ever have to introduce myself to someone ever again, I could just say "I'm . . ." and then play back his mellow radio announcer's version of "Cody."

All that goes through my head in the two seconds it takes me to reach out my hand. His grip is gentle. That tells me he's been raised Indian. One of the first things my father taught me—mostly just by doing it—was the right way to shake hands among our people. When Indian men shake hands, they never make it a contest of strength. They don't try to prove how tough they are like so many non-Indian guys do by trying to crush the other person's paw. You just relax your hand in the other person's grasp.

I look up at his face. The smile's still there, as well as an attentive look that tells me he's waiting for whatever I'm about to say. I quickly look down. Meeting someone's eyes and holding them is disrespectful—just the opposite of how it is in the Anglo world.

"*Kwai, kwai*, Uncle," I say in Abenaki. "*Oli*. It is good that you are here. I am glad."

"*Kwai, kwai*, Nephew," he answers me, his right hand letting go of mine and sliding down to take my wrist in an old-style handshake. "*Oli*. I am glad to be here."

As he takes my wrist and I grasp his, his sleeve falls back and I notice not just how muscular his forearm is, but also the tattoo on the inside of it. I've never seen a design like it before. It's the paw of a bear with a circle inside its palm. And within that circle is another circle that is half black and half white. Like two fat exclamation points nestled together.

Uncle John releases his grip on my wrist and turns his

45

palm up. He points at the tattoo with the little finger of his left hand.

"This is me," he says, cocking his head toward me as if to make sure I am paying attention.

His little finger traces the outline of the bear paw. "*Awassos*. Bear. My name and my clan." He jerks his chin in my direction. "Yours, too." I nod, and his finger continues to the design with the bear's paw. "The circle inside the bear paw, that's what is all around us."

I don't quite understand that. I know I should. But I don't nod.

Uncle John looks at me. "You don't understand that? *Oli*. Good. First, because the less you know, the more you learn. Second, it tells me you believe in telling the truth. If you say that you know what you don't know, then you may never know."

He chuckles at my even more visible confusion as his finger comes to rest on the night-and-day-colored design at the center of his tattoo.

"And this?" he asks.

"I think it's a Chinese symbol," I answer.

"*Ktsi oli*, very good! Yin and yang." He pulls his sleeve back over his arm. "That's enough for now."

"Are you just visiting?" I ask. It's no longer the hostile question it would have been only five minutes ago.

Mom has come up closer now and has her hand on my shoulder.

"If it's okay with you and your mother," Uncle John says, "I'm going to be camping out here for a while."

"If Cody doesn't mind," Mom says.

I look at her. Why is she dumping this on my shoulders? Much as I'm starting to like this new uncle, I'm not really sure I want him staying with us. This is all happening too fast. But I also know what Mom wants to hear.

"It's okay." I shrug my shoulders. "We've got plenty of room."

The half-cough/half-laugh that Mom tries not to let out from behind my back reminds me how ridiculous that last statement of mine is. Our trailer is so small that Uncle John's head is almost scraping the ceiling. Just yesterday I'd been complaining that I didn't have any elbowroom.

But I can't retreat now. "I could sleep on the couch, I guess. Then you could use my bedroom."

"Cody," Mom says. "Thank you for being so generous. But are you sure?"

"It's okay," I answer. I nod. Maybe one or two times too many.

Uncle John grasps my shoulder. "Thanks," he says. "But let's not make any quick decisions. We can talk about this at dinner. I'd like to take you and my big sister here out for a bite to eat. Okay!"

"Okay," I agree. Maybe I'm not going to have to give up my room after all. "Dinner sounds good."

"Better wash your face first," Mom says. "And change your shirt. The one you like is on top of the laundry basket."

In the bathroom I look at myself in our mirror that is so old it is half frosted over, and my reflection is all blurred at the edges. I can see clearly enough, though. My nose is still swollen, and I realize that Uncle John must have noticed the blood that was caked under my left nostril and the stains on my plaid shirt where I bled all over it. What must I have looked like to him?

I wash my face and drop the stained shirt into the wicker laundry hamper that takes up half the space inside our midget bathroom where you bang your knees on the sink getting up from the toilet and you have to bend over like a contortionist to get into the shower. All of the excitement I'd been feeling has escaped from me like a wild bird that just strayed into your room and then escaped out the open window.

Even if Uncle John is as cool a person as he seems to be, the kind of uncle every guy might like to have, it isn't going to take him long to recognize me for who I truly am. He may think he likes me now, but wait until he gets to know the real me.

Cody LeBeau, the loser.

Chapter 7

GIVE ME YOUR HAND

The bird's flight follows
the path of the sky.
—Master Net

We've gotten halfway through dinner and I haven't said anything stupid. Amazingly.

It's been easier than I expected, despite the fact that I came out of my room absolutely certain that I was about to embarrass myself in front of my new uncle. Especially because I wanted so much to show him that I was someone he'd like to have as a nephew. I've discovered that whenever I try really hard to do something, I tend to goof it up. My recent karate class fiasco being a case in point.

After years of watching martial arts in movies and on TV and reading every book on the subject that I could get my hands on, I finally took a free after-school karate class

49

last week at the Y. And I sucked big-time.

It wasn't just that I couldn't do anything right. I was so awful that I couldn't even do anything wrong! When the sensei tried to show me how to take the horse stance, I kept losing my balance. Whenever I attempted a kick, I ended up on my back. And when I tried doing a *Ki-yah*, the yell that you do when you throw a strike, I sounded like a rabbit with a hernia. I even managed to punch myself in the face and give myself such a bloody nose that I had to sit out the last half of the class. You should have heard the other kids laugh when that happened. Even after the sensei told them to stop, some were still snickering at me.

Karate brings together a balance of body and mind. Yeah, sure. Except I proved myself to be the kid who doesn't have either one. The few Japanese words Sensei DiGiorno tried to teach me kept jumping out of my head, even though I knew I'd heard most of them already with all the stuff I'd watched over the years—not to mention all the reading I'd done.

As I trudged home that evening, I made one of my mental memos to self: *Find a garbage bag large enough to hold two shelves of books on the martial arts, arranged alphabetically from Aikido to Wing Chung Kung Fu.* I knew there was no way I could ever, not in a million years, attend that karate class again. Like I said, the perfect recipe for me messing up is for me to really want to succeed.

But dinner has actually been fun so far. Going out to eat turned out to be staying in. We're having dinner right here in our trailer, which is just fine by me. In part it's because this is the first time I've been able to sit down for dinner with Mom in ages. Usually at this time of the evening, she is off to work, and I'm nuking something she's left for me in the fridge and trying to find something worth watching on the four channels we can get on our hundred-year-old, non-cable-connected, thirteen-inch TV that's so old that its white plastic case is sort of melting around the edges of the screen.

But not tonight. Mom has gotten permission to go to work later than usual. And the food is really good. Really different, too. Uncle John, it turns out, is a great cook. In no time at all, he made us some kind of stir-fry and then served it with brown rice. Yes! He's brought a sack full of things with him, not just the main ingredients like the rice and the tofu and veggies, but also spices and oils and even a personal wok—his own private cooking pan—that he told us he always travels with. It is black cast iron and not coated with Teflon, which he said isn't good for your health.

"Traditional ways are often the best," he says with that cool smile of his. "That's why I always like to take an old-fashioned wok."

Both Mom and I groan at that pun. Most kids might

not have gotten it, but Mom likes songs from old movies, and she's always humming that one that goes, "Let's take an old-fashioned walk . . ."

It's so easy with Uncle John here, the three of us around the table. Not tense like it was whenever "the three of us" meant Dad and Mom and me. As I think that, I feel guilty. Why did I feel tense when my father was here? Am I being disloyal to him by liking my new uncle, whom I never even knew about before today? I can feel the clouds settling around my head again. They're thick and gray with rain. The rain is cold and so heavy that I can't see through the darkness. I'm plodding along down a dark road with no end in sight, my feet slogging through the mud that is sucking my feet into it . . .

"Cody." Uncle John's voice pulls me back from whatever depth I'm sinking into. How can he do that just by saying my name? I look up at him.

He makes a little circling gesture, ending with his right hand being held out toward me. Cool! I imagine myself making that same gesture. In fact, I move my hand, which is below the table where I'm sure he can't see it, in what I think is that same gesture. But I'm wrong on both counts.

"Give me your hand," he says, reaching both hands toward me.

I pull my hand from under the table, and he takes it in both of his.

"Now relax."

I let my arm and hand go limp, and he guides them through the gesture he's just done, a circle that begins with an open palm held out—like you're telling someone to stop—and then ends with that same hand palm up, as if you're holding something in it.

"Now, you do it."

I move my hand the way he showed me, and I'm amazed. For a moment it looks almost as graceful as his hand did, more like a bird in flight than one of my clumsy paws. As soon as I think that, my hand movement gets jerky. I slam my wrist into my half-empty water glass and knock it right off the table.

"Oh no!" I blurt out, closing my eyes. Our old brown carpet is so worn and thin that I know it won't cushion the impact. I brace myself for the sound of shattering glass. But I don't hear that. All I hear is a word.

"Cody."

I open my eyes. I blink. I can't believe it. Uncle John is holding the glass I just knocked off the table. It's even still half full. I feel as if I should say something. *Thank you? How the heck did you do that?*

But I just stare.

Uncle John nods and puts the glass down in front of me.

"Try it again," he says. "Take a deep breath. You're doing fine."

I take a deep breath. I'm doing fine. I will try it again.

But first I pick up the water glass and take a big drink from it. I need to check that I'm awake and not having some kind of dream. The water is real. I taste the minerals in it and feel it going down my throat. I carefully put the glass down—on the other side of my plate this time—and slowly, carefully, try to repeat that hand gesture.

"*Oli*," Uncle John says. "Good. Now just feel the air as you do that. Do it without trying to do it right."

I don't understand what he means, but it works. My circling motion gets easier and lighter. It's as if my hand doesn't belong to me anymore, but also as if my hand is more my own than it's ever been before. It's moving faster, but I'm not consciously making it speed up. I feel the air. It makes me feel as if I am almost floating up from my chair as I do it. Finally I let my hand flutter down to rest on the table.

"*Ktsi oli*, Cody," Uncle John says. He reaches back to pick up a cup from the counter in the kitchen nook behind us. Easy enough to do in a trailer that's only about as wide as his big shoulders.

"Second step," he says. He balances the cup on his palm, pours water from his glass into it, and then—don't ask me how—he actually circles his hand all the way around on his wrist so the cup is carried under his arm, up toward the ceiling, and then back again where he started. Without spilling a drop.

"The Student offers the Master a cup of tea," he says, as if that was some kind of explanation. "But don't try that yet." He puts the cup down. "Anyhow, I'm getting way ahead of myself. Let's back up."

He looks over at Mom.

"As your Uncle John said, he'd like to stay with us for a while. If you are sure that it's okay with you," she says.

Yes! I think. I also intend to say it, but my tongue doesn't seem to want to work. So I just do my typical idiotic head nod—three or four times like one of those toy drinking birds you balance on the edge of a glass.

"You don't have to give up your room, Nephew," Uncle John says. "Though it was generous of you to offer. When I said I'd be camping out, I meant just that. I've got all of my gear stowed behind the trailer. I can set up my tent back there under those little cedars. I'll be out of sight and I'll be comfortable. In fact I've gotten so used to sleeping outside that I prefer it. My sleeping bag is good for forty-below. I just need to use your facilities, take a shower now and then, keep my toothbrush and my razor in the medicine cabinet."

Sleeping outside under the stars. How cool is that? That's something Dad always said that we ought to do one day, just the three of us, go camping together. When he was home for any length of time from his trucking work and when I wasn't in school and when we had enough money to buy a tent and some sleeping bags. Lots of "whens." But never any "nows."

Mom and Uncle John are both looking at me and waiting. I drag myself back and nod at them. It's fine if he camps out back. But then I think about what that means, staying in a tent. To me, even in a tent in our tiny backyard, camping out means staying just a little while. Like over the weekend.

My voice comes back to me. "How long?" I ask.

"About ten weeks," Uncle John says, "if that's not too long—"

"Why ten weeks?" I blurt out before he's even finished his sentence.

"Because that's when the big tournament takes place," Uncle John says, as if it explains everything. "The War by the Shore."

I look at him blankly.

Then he lifts his big right hand, spreads his fingers wide, and slowly curls them into a fist, knuckles cracking as he does.

"I'm a fighter," he says.

And, all of a sudden, I understand.

Chapter 8

OUR DEAL

To climb a mountain
take one small step.
—Pendetta Satu

I'm in bed, but I can't sleep. I look over at the clock on my nightstand. The lighted digital display reads 1:00 A.M. What started and kept going as a lousy day has turned around so drastically that my head is spinning and I'm wide awake. I can't wait for it to be morning.

My bedroom is the one with the window, high up on the wall, that looks out on our little twenty-foot-by-thirty-foot backyard. Mom tried making it into a garden, but it was so shaded by the cedar trees and the trailer that nothing survived but weeds. Until our visitor arrived, the only things we had out there were a couple of pots with dead flowers in them, a rickety wooden picnic table, and a tool shed not much bigger than one of the lockers at school.

I push back the covers and get up on my knees to look out the window. I can see the top of Uncle John's tent, but that's it. We set it up after cleaning up the dinner dishes and seeing Mom off to work, both of us waving to her as she backed her '94 Toyota out the driveway and then took off to the usual accompaniment of knocking rods.

"Tomorrow," Uncle John said, "I need to do a little work on that engine."

Then, because it was already almost eight o'clock and getting dark, we turned on the back light and went to put up his tent. In fact, I did most of it myself. It was really easy because it's one of those tents that open up sort of like an umbrella. What took the longest time was unpacking and getting organized—which Uncle John did with great care and slow deliberation, one item at a time.

"Get organized before you get going," he said. Those were his exact words. When I got back into my room, I wrote them down in my earth science notebook. (Lots of empty pages in there.)

It was amazing how much equipment he had in his back-pack and his two duffel bags. Not only did he have a ground cloth and the tent, a foam pad, his sleeping bag and his pillow, but he also had a little fold-up canvas chair, a lantern, and a whole tool kit, including such things as a combination hatchet and hammer and different-sized wrenches and screwdrivers—which were in the top of the first bag he opened. In fact, one of the first things he did when we went out into the backyard was to use that tool kit to fix our old picnic table so he could spread his things out on it.

Of course, I haven't finished listing all the things he unpacked. There were his clothes. But not a lot of those. Aside from what he wore—black jeans and a loose, long-sleeved hoodie with a black T-shirt under it—he had only three changes of clothes that were exactly the same as what he had on, plus two pairs of sweat pants and one shirt pat-terned like a Pendleton blanket, the kind they put around someone's shoulders during an honoring ceremony. As far as footwear went, in addition to the boots he was wearing, he had a set of cross-trainer New Balance sneakers and a pair of black highly polished dress shoes. And, of course, he had extra socks and hankies and underwear. What else was there? Two towels, two washcloths, and two black ball caps, one plain and one of them with a bulldog and the words "The Gracie Way" on it. His entire wardrobe made just three small, neat piles on top of the picnic table.

"Look at all this clothing," he said. "I surely do drag a lot around with me. In some of the places I've been, only a wealthy man could have this big a wardrobe."

Was he kidding? Even *I* owned ten times as many clothes as this! He saw the skeptical look on my face.

"Did you know that John Muir hiked across America for years with nothing but the clothes he wore and a paper bag to carry a change of underwear?"

I didn't. "Wow," I said. I also made one of my mental notes to self: *Find out more about John Muir.*

What else did he have? A shaving kit and a pretty sizable bag that had everything from bandages to vitamins and bottles labeled in what I guess was Chinese. He had a wicked wrist-rocket slingshot.

"Good as a bow and arrow at short range," he explained. "Rabbit, turkey, grouse." He slapped the lock-blade knife that hung in its sheath on his belt. "Plus a good knife to dress your game." While he was camping out as he hitched his way here, he'd pretty much fed himself on whatever he could forage or hunt when he was in the countryside. "And in every city," he said, "there's always free food to be had if you know how to dive."

That confused me a little. I didn't know you could get food by diving.

The one bag he didn't open was the one I was most curious about. He'd let me carry it over to the tent after we got it set up, and it was heavy. He carefully placed it in the back of the tent.

"Training gear," he said. "I'll show you what I have tomorrow."

Then he sat down in his folding canvas chair and gestured for me to take a seat at the picnic table.

"So," he said. "Remember what part of our deal is?"

I nodded and felt my heart start to pound. I was both pumped up with anticipation and feeling my usual doubts about being able to do anything right. The deal about Uncle John's staying with us while he was training for the big mixed-martial-arts tournament at the Koacook Casino was that he would pay for his room and board. He would do this not just with whatever money he could earn doing odd jobs, but also by helping us out. Fixing the picnic table, doing repair work around the trailer—which really needed a lot of that—and getting Mom's car running right. And part of that deal was that he would try to repair the one thing around the house that is truly a hopeless case. Me.

Uncle John had agreed to teach me whatever he could about the martial arts.

A hundred scenarios ran through my head. Would he be like Mr. Miyagi in *The Karate Kid* and have me do things like painting or building a deck, simple everyday motions that would build muscle memory and strength and would translate into lightning-fast proficiency in blocking and punching? Or would he fasten weights to my legs and tell me to jump up and down, adding more and more weights each day until the day came when he took them off and I found myself able to leap right over the tops of buildings? Maybe he'd just start off by having me punching and kicking sandbags and heavy beams of wood until my knuckles were broken and bleeding, all the while building devastating power.

Whatever he did, Uncle John was sure to do something dramatic that would demonstrate the great power of his style to me. All the old kung fu teachers in the movies did that.

Master, how can that crane hand be effective against an enemy attack?

Hah, foolish student. Observe.

Then the master pulverizes a concrete wall with his crane-hand strike.

Then it came to me. I didn't have a concrete wall, but I did have some boards! Soon after we'd moved in, I'd found a six-foot-long, twelve-inch-wide board under the trailer. With the rusty saw I found in the tool shed, I'd cut it into six pieces. Then I'd tried to break one of those twelve-inch-square pieces with a punch. All I had succeeded in doing was to bruise my knuckles. Uncle John, though, would be able to do it easily. Breaking boards. That was it! It'd be a great way for him to show me the effectiveness of his martial art. Then he could teach me how to break a board.

I jumped up from the picnic table. Uncle John held up his hand, but I shook my head.

"I'll be right back," I said.

I ran to where I'd shoved the boards behind the shed, pulled them out, and came running back, but not before dropping half of them on the way and having to turn back to pick them up again.

I put them on top of the table.

"Here," I said, looking eagerly at Uncle John.

He got up from his chair, walked over to the table, and sat across from me. He picked up the top board and studied it.

"Good," he said. "We can make a birdhouse out of these."

He put the board down on the stack.

"Aren't you going to break it?" I asked.

He shook his head. "You get a cleaner edge with a saw."

"But . . . ," I couldn't think what to say.

He held up his hand. "It's not about breaking boards."

I felt my face getting red. I'd already proven myself to be a total idiot. He already could see I'm hopeless.

Instead, he grinned at me. "Cody," he said, "looking at you is like looking into a mirror. You're just as impatient as I was when I was your age." He tapped the pile of boards with his little finger. "And thinking about breaking boards isn't stupid. Chuck Lidell says that breaking has helped him build up the power. That's how he won the Ultimate Fighting Championship. Ever see one of his fights? Those big, wide, kempo hooks that he throws? But you don't *start* there. That's not how it is with The Way. The way to start learning The Way is to stop. Stop trying so hard. Stop hurrying." Uncle John chuckled. "And right about now my old teacher would be telling me to stop talking."

Uncle John picked up the boards and put them under the table. When he lifted his hand back up, he was holding a stone that had a sharp edge on it, so sharp that when he scraped it on the surface of the wooden table, it cut a circle. Just about a perfect circle—which, as anyone can tell you, is almost impossible to draw freehand.

"This is what it's about," he said. "The Circle. The Way. I don't just mean that in terms of martial arts. The Way is part of our heritage, part of our blood. Our ancestors tried to live by The Way. In The Way, everything is a circle, and everything is connected. Nothing in creation is outside of it. No person is left out. Everything is perfect, and everything is in balance. We all know that in our hearts, but we fight it. We get frightened, and then we think we either have to fight or run away. Adrenalin takes over. We let our thoughts confuse us. So what I want to teach you is how to teach yourself. How to find your way back to The Way."

My own hand had reached out to trace its way around that circle. I felt calmer doing it, calmer hearing his words, which were spoken so softly I could barely hear them.

"Okay," I said.

"Tomorrow," Uncle John said, "we begin. Tomorrow we teach you how to breathe. But now," he said, looking at his watch, "it's time for you to go to bed. I promised your mother I'd make sure you hit the hay before midnight."

Tomorrow I'll learn how to breathe.

It's already tomorrow, and I'm already breathing. It seems as if half of what Uncle John says is a riddle and the other half is so simple that anyone can understand it. I look at the clock. 1:30 A.M. now. I start to lie back down, and then I hear something. Not that loud. It's a quick snapping sound coming from out back. I stand up on my bed again and grab the bottom of the windowsill to pull myself up as high as I can. Now I can see into the yard. Uncle John is sitting at the picnic table. His hammer is next to him, and he's laid out a line of nails. He's holding up one of my boards in one hand and looking at it. Then he places his other hand with his fingertips on the board and the heel of his hand an inch away.

Whap! The heel of his hand has snapped forward so fast that I hardly saw it move. And the board he hit—and caught before it struck the ground—has been broken in half as cleanly along the grain as if it had been cut with a saw.

Chapter 9

RUNNING

Even the fastest runner
can never escape his shadow.
—Sensei Ni

Even on a dark and rainy day, I know when it is almost sunrise. Dad said it was part of my genetic make-up. Our ancestors always made it a point to greet the new day, welcome the sun and say "thank you" for its giving us the gifts of life and light.

So it's no hardship at all for me to do what Uncle John asked me to do: meet him in the backyard at dawn. That way we'll have more than half an hour for him to start teaching me before Mom gets back from her overnight shift. Then we can have breakfast together before I have to catch the bus.

The first thing I see when I step out back is a new birdhouse. Made from some of those boards I brought out to

Uncle John. It's sitting on the picnic table next to that old saw I found. But the saw no longer looks old. It's been oiled, and its teeth look at if they've been sharpened. I remember the files my uncle had in his toolkit. I must have slept sounder than I thought not to have heard him out here filing the saw, cutting the wood, and then nailing that birdhouse together. How late did he stay up after I went to bed?

And where is he? The flap of his tent is open, his sleeping bag is neatly rolled up, but there's no sign of him. Then I hear someone whistle from the other side of the trailer—not one of those "here, boy" dog whistles, but the long, sharp whistle like a red-tailed hawk's call. I open the gate in the gray, sagging stockade fence that encloses the backyard and look out front. Uncle John is standing there in the road, motioning to me to join him. Well, not really standing. Jogging in place. Early as I woke up, he woke up earlier.

I close the gate behind me and run over to him. He's wearing his hoodie and one of those pairs of sweat pants, and the cross-trainers are on his feet. He looks as if he's just done a five-mile run. There's sweat on his face, and he has that warm glow about him that runners get.

"We can get a good two miles in if we hustle," he says. "Run to greet the sun."

I look at myself. Run? I can barely walk without stumbling. Plus my sneakers are a wreck, and I don't have any sweats. He must be kidding. There's a little smile on his face, though, as he gestures toward the trailer with his chin.

"On the table," he says. "Hurry up and change."

I almost rip the flimsy screen door off the hinges getting into the trailer. Oh man! There on the table on top of a hoodie and sweat pants is a new pair of shoes—New Balance cross-trainers just like his. My size. He must have had them inside that bag of his that he didn't open. I yank off my old sneaks without even untying them, strip off my clothes, and put everything on. There's not time to go into the bathroom and look at myself in the mirror, but I feel as if I look like somebody totally different.

I open the door and jump from the top step down to the ground. The new sneakers cushion my feet, and I hardly feel the pavement when I land. It's not like walking on rocks like it was with my old worn-out shoes. I'm running on air.

"We start slow," Uncle John says. "Don't think about running. Just breathe."

He turns and jogs down the edge of the road, and I follow him for the first fifty yards or so until he turns his head back toward me and gestures for me forward to run next to him.

"Breathe," he says again.

We run and we keep running. I can hear his breath and try to match mine with his. Slow and even. A hundred yards, two hundred yards.

This is so easy, I think. *I could run forever*. And as soon as I think that, I feel a tightening in my chest. My breath is no longer smooth but ragged. My feet aren't floating—they're thudding against the ground.

"Look up. Breathe. Don't use your feet. Relax. Let each breath pull you further along. Just one breath. Then another."

It's easier to say something like that than it is to do it, a stubborn voice inside me says. I know that quitter's voice. But for once I don't let it tell me what to do. Instead I answer it with my uncle's words. *Relax. Just one breath. Then another. Just one breath. Then another.*

"Hy!" Uncle John swings his arm to his right and dives off the road onto a trail that leads downhill into the park. It's so quick a turn than I almost stumble, but I keep my feet and fly down the hill after him. He's just ahead of me on the path that is too narrow for us to run abreast. We're going around trees, up and down hills at the same even pace. I almost don't make it up the last hill, but when I see that he's stopped at the top, I keep going until I reach him. I'm still breathing, but I'm gasping now like a goldfish that has flipped out of its tank onto the floor.

"Straight," he says, putting one hand on my back and another on my chest. "Bend your knees a little. Now lift your hands like this and breathe in. Good. Now breathe out as you bring your hands down. Keep doing it as you close your eyes. Just your breath. Nothing but your breath. *In.* And *out.* Slow your breath. *In.* And *out.* Slow down your heartbeat. *In.* And *out.* *In.* And *out.*"

I do as he says and can't believe how it works. Although my breath trembles the first time I draw it in, it's smoother when I let it out and from then on it gets easier each time. My heart, which was thudding like a bird hurling its frantic body against the bars of a cage, actually does slow its beat. And each time I breathe in, I can feel the smile on my face get broader. I can't remember when I've felt this good before.

"Good," Uncle John says. "Very good. Now open your eyes, Cody. Greet our oldest friend."

I open my eyes and realize that the hill we've climbed is facing east. There, just starting to show itself above the low range of hills, is the thin, gold crescent of Kisos, the sun.

Uncle John holds out his arms as if to embrace that first light, and I do the same. I feel the warmth of the new day touching my face and embracing me right back, not just holding me but flowing into me.

"*Oliohneh,*" Uncle John says to the sun. "Thank you."

He nods to me and then we say it together.

"*Oliohneh.*"

On our way back, we alternate jogging and walking.

Uncle John also shows me some runner's stretches. "Best to do these before you run,'" he says. "But this morning what you needed most was to run without thinking about it."

I nod. But what I am thinking about is how far we actually ran. It was at least a mile, maybe more. It's further than I've ever run before. And I did it! When we get back to the house, Mom is already there waiting for us.

The first thing Mom does is compliment me.

"You look great, kiddo!" she says.

"You, too, kiddo," I crack back. But I mean it. Mom usually looks drained when she gets home from one of those long nights, but this morning she looks fresh as the proverbial daisy.

"Wise guy!" She pokes me in the ribs, but the smile on her face tells me that she's feeling pretty good, too. "Now hurry up and change. There's barely time for you to get a bite to eat before the bus gets here."

I change out of the sweats but not the sneakers. No way am I ever going to put those old scruffies back on my feet again.

When I get back to the table, only Mom is there. I can see the tiredness is starting to catch up with her now. It's visible first in her eyes; then it works its way to her mouth. Exhaustion is this heavy weight dragging her down. But she still smiles at me. She always does that.

"Where's Uncle John?" I ask.

"He said to tell you he had to finish his road work. He needs to get in another ten miles of running before he goes over to the gym."

Ten more miles of running? And I thought our run to that hilltop and back was a big deal!

"Your nose isn't swollen anymore," Mom says, gently touching my face.

I lean back from her. The last thing I want is to be reminded of what happened in school yesterday.

"It really isn't," Mom says. "And that black eye will probably be gone in a day or two."

Black eye! What black eye? I jump up from the table and run into the bathroom. In the hazy glass of the mirror, I see it. The swelling may have left my nose, but it has migrated into my eye socket, which is all purple. I look like a raccoon with half a mask! Great! Just great! I may have been running this morning, but there's no way I can ever get away from who I am. A beat-up wimp.

Chapter 10

PAYING ATTENTION

Eyes closed,
Is the world still there?
—Sifu Sahn

For once, fortune is smiling on me. Grey Cook isn't on the bus this morning. I've gotten so used to his picking on me that I almost miss hearing his sarcastic voice when I climb on the bus.

I relax back in my seat. Perfect! I close my eyes and start thinking about the last thing that Uncle John said to me this morning about breathing and staying calm.

"It all begins with breath," he'd said. "When you get frightened or worried, your breath gets quick and shallow. And the faster you breathe, the harder it is to breathe. If you want to stay calm, breathe slowly. *In*. And *out*. Pay attention to your breath. Before long, your breath will take over and start breathing you."

Without a skinny, bad-tempered junior jerk ragging on me, I actually am able to think about something other than just praying for the bus ride to end this morning. I'm able to truly pay attention to my breathing. *In*. And *out*. Making my breath even and long. Making it into a circle. In through my nose, down deep into my lungs to the center of my body, below my belly button.

I can't remember the name Uncle John called it, but it's the center of balance and breath down there. Pay attention. Breathe down to that place. Down, down. That's it. A word like "down." *Dan. Dan chien.* Down to the *dan chien* and then back up the other side of the circle and out my mouth.

I'm concentrating so much on breathing that I am hardly aware of the other kids getting onto the bus. In fact, I don't even notice how long the usually endless ride takes. All of a sudden the bus is stopped, and everyone is getting out. We're at the school.

I get off the bus, still breathing. I go through the doors, and this morning the doors don't throw me off-balance when I try to get through them. I just breathe, step, push easy, and they swing open. No sweat.

Maybe it was the run and greeting the sun, or maybe it's just the breathing, but I feel really awake this morning. I actually feel . . . could it be? I feel *good*. I am in school and feeling good. I'm not even thinking about my black eye.

Ooops! Yes, I am now. *Breathe, Cody. Keep breathing.*

I breathe my way down the hall. Nobody runs into me, by accident or accidentally on purpose. I make it unbruised to my locker, put my bag inside, and pull out the books and notebook for my first class. I keep breathing as I walk. Now I'm through the door of my homeroom. Now I am in the chair in the back of the room and sitting up straight.

Roll call starts. Here comes my name.

"Mr. Leee-booo?" mispronouncing my name as usual.

Then it happens. I don't mumble my usual surly, "Here." Instead I hear a clear, self-assured voice saying my teacher's name. And that person is me!

"Ms. Taker?"

"Yes, Cody?"

"The way to pronounce my name is *Luh-Bow.* Could you please say it that way?"

Ms. Taker is taken aback. Then she lifts her index finger up to her chin in an "oh, I never realized that" gesture.

"Oh," she says. "I'm sorry, Cody. *Luh-Bow,* it is. In fact," she says and smiles brightly, "I believe that means 'the handsome one' in French."

I take a breath. I don't put my head down like I usually do. I think about the sound of Uncle John's voice.

"I can take it if you can," I say. My words come out confident and pleasant. Almost cool. Ms. Taker actually smiles at me before she moves on down the roll to call the next name.

"Snap," someone whispers a few seats ahead and two rows over from me. Then she giggles. I look over. It's Maya, who is looking over her shoulder at me. She lifts up two fingers to make an invisible mark in the air—score one point for LeBeau—before she turns back.

As Ms. Taker continues calling the roll, I dare to quickly look around at the rest of the class. Nobody is staring at me. Aside from Maya's affirmation, no one has made a big deal out of my speaking up. No one even seems to have noticed my black eye. It's as if my not thinking about it has made it invisible. Made *me* invisible.

It makes me start wondering what it is that makes people aware of each other. Every day we pass by so many people without even thinking about it. Like have you ever noticed how when you're driving down the road, passing car after car going the other way, you never really see the faces of the people in those other cars. But if you deliberately look at the face of one of those people in the front seat—a driver or another passenger like you—more often than not, they'll know it. They'll make eye contact with you in that split second before you whiz past each other. Weird.

And then I remember something I read in an issue of *Black Belt* magazine. It was an article about ninjas, those semi-supernatural assassins of ancient Japan. It was said that they could slip in anywhere without being seen, make themselves invisible. Maybe it wasn't real invisibility, like in *The Lord of the Rings*. Maybe it was just that they knew what to do—how to move, how to breathe, even how to think. People *thought* they were invisible. They just knew how to do things without drawing attention to themselves.

Just as I am thinking that, something draws my attention. I sense more than see something way off to my left. A disturbance in the Force, to use an overworked *Stars Wars* metaphor. It's like there's a black cloud over there. Without moving my head, I shift my eyes toward the other back corner of the room and see the look on Jackson Teeter's face. It's a look of pure hatred, not directed at me, but at the front of the class where Ms. Taker has her back turned. He's nodding to the beat of whatever death-rock group he's imprinted in the digital memory of the MP3 player that's jammed into a front pocket of his flak jacket. Then Stump lifts up his right hand, points his index finger at our teacher, lifts his thumb, and drops it down like the hammer of a gun as he mouths a word.

Bang.

Chapter 11

NEED TO KNOW

The wise man knows what he knows.
The sage knows what he does not.
—Sifu Sahn

"How many people does this seat?" I ask.

Mom and Uncle John and I are standing at the top of the huge new stadium-style arena at Koacook Moon. We're looking down the endless rows of seats cut by aisles that radiate up from the center like bicycle spokes. Aside from some maintenance men sweeping the floor below, we're the only people in the place.

"Eighteen thousand screaming fight fans," Uncle John answers me in a drawl that's an imitation of either Michael or Bruce Buffer, the two brothers who've become the most famous fight announcers of the twenty-first century.

In the center of the arena, an eight-sided ring surrounded by metal netting about eight feet high has been set up.

"That's where it'll take place?" I ask. A dumb question that my uncle actually dignifies with an answer.

"In the Octagon," he says. "Too bad I'm an Abenaki and not a Navajo, or I'd feel right at home in there."

The three of us smile. Indian humor. The traditional homes of Navajo people are eight-sided buildings called hogans. We Abenakis lived in round wigwams.

"Better hurry," Mom says. "We're supposed to be there at seven P.M."

I'm not sure who we're meeting for dinner. I don't even know who got the invitation, Mom or Uncle John. But all three of us have been included. Uncle John has loaned me a bolo tie to go with my best blue shirt. Aside from the fact that his shirt has embroidery around the sleeves and the pockets, he and I are dressed the same, from our cross-trainer sneakers on up to our twin bolos with a bear design in the center of the beadwork.

"My two guys," Mom says as she links her arms between us. Hearing her say those words tugged at my heart. On the one hand, it makes me feel taller. On the other hand, she used those exact words the last time she and Dad and I went out together. Three years and 4TPA.

Leaving the arena, we walk down a hallway lined with pictures of the members of the Tribal Council and their families. I find myself recognizing some of those faces.

They either look like kids I've seen in the halls or, in some cases, are those exact kids themselves. Like the one we just passed of none other than Jeff Chahna. In full football uniform.

I reach up to my eye and study my reflection in the glass that covers Jeff Chahna's photo. Even though it was three weeks ago, I still remember him punching me as if it was yesterday. Of course, my eye's not even tender anymore, and the discoloration is long gone. It usually takes at least a week before you look normal again after getting a black eye. (Trust me on that, years of experience.) But this time it only took three days for it to disappear. Maybe because of all the running, deep breathing, and other physical activities Uncle John had me doing.

"Take care of your body and it will return the favor by taking care of you," he said just yesterday.

Then he rolled up the right leg of his sweat pants and showed me the network of scars around his knee. "Courtesy of an IED, improvised explosive device. They said I'd need a whole knee replacement or I'd never walk again. But my body said something different. With the aid of half a year of physical therapy."

That's the closest Uncle John has come to telling me anything about his experiences as a Marine. I've asked him twice about it. The first time was when I got home from school the second night of his stay.

"What was it like in Iraq?" I asked.

"Cody," he said, "you don't need to know."

End of subject.

The second time was a week later.

"Can you tell me anything about your experiences as a Marine?" The same question, of course, but different words.

And he answered the same, but used different words. Because that time he waited a good, long time, just sitting there silently before saying, "Cody, you *really* don't need to know."

Mental note to self: *Do NOT ask that question again.*

Uncle John doesn't limp even a little on that leg that was so badly injured. And he runs twelve miles every morning and spends another five or six hours in the local gym every day. He boxes and wrestles with some of the other men who are working out there, plus he does free weights. And after all that, he never seems too tired to spend time with me. Nothing has ever seemed to bother him.

Until just now.

"How many more miles till we get there?" Uncle John asks as we continue down that endless hallway. It's a humorous remark, but I can sense a tone in his voice I haven't heard before. Is he actually nervous? I shake my head. He can't be. Not Uncle John.

Mom pats his arm. "It's okay, John," she says. It's a

similar gesture and tone of voice she's used with me when I'm sure the world is going to collapse around my ears. I want to ask where we are going. I need to know what the big deal is and why we're here heading toward the casino's big dining room. But I don't ask.

"Here we are," Mom says in a voice that sounds strained. Jeesum Crow! She's nervous, too. What is going on?

We walk into the dining room where the maître d' comes right up to us before anyone can say anything. He's probably seen Mom countless times before because she works here sometimes waiting tables. But he acts as if she is royalty.

"This way, madam," he says, with a little half-bow. "They're already at the table."

Mom lifts her head, like it is no big deal, and sails after him. We follow, but not before I really look at my mother, trying to imagine how someone who doesn't know her might see her. And I realize how great she looks tonight. I've never seen that dress or the jewelry she's wearing, and she found time sometime today to get her hair done.

We go around the corner of a room divider erected to create a private dining area with only two tables in front of a huge window looking out over the shore of the lake. The best seats in the house. A big Koacook guy who has to be in his forties gets up from his seat. He's wearing a tailored Italian suit that makes the clothes Uncle John and I are wearing look out of place. But there's a big smile on the man's face, and he is reaching out to my mother.

"Louise," he says, taking her hand and holding it for what seems to me like too long a time. "I am so glad you're here. Let me introduce you to my son. I don't think you've met him before."

He reaches toward the young man who is also standing up. He's wearing a suit, too, and looks like a slightly less-wide copy of his father, who is the tribal chairman of the Koacook Nation.

Maybe Mom hasn't met him before, but I have. And so has my nose.

"I'm pleased to meet you," Jeff Chahna says.

Chapter 12

NO STYLE

Do nothing, see nothing.
Want nothing, find nothing.
—Master Net

So much happened during that dinner that it's as hard for me to understand it. Even now, twenty-four hours later, I'm still a little confused.

I guess I can get back to all that later. Here's where I am today.

In terms of learning The Way, even after three weeks of unlearning bad habits, I am still a long way away. Right now, I'm standing on one leg, my back straight, my weight-bearing knee slightly bent, my hands drawn back to my side in the chamber position. I'm trying to relax and stay in balance and not think about the pain I'm feeling in my calf.

"Stop trying," Uncle John says from behind me. "Be nowhere."

The first time he said that was after we'd been training together for a week. His first week of basic lessons might have seemed weird to someone who hadn't read as much as I have about the martial arts over the past six years. What he was teaching me to do were the things that everyone does every day. The big four, as he called them: Breathing, Walking (which includes running), Listening, and Seeing. Yes, I know, every two-year-old kid knows how to do all four of those things.

"In fact," Uncle John said, "most two-year-old kids breathe and walk and listen and see better than adults or even teenagers. That's because they realize they are learning. They're paying attention to the world around them. They haven't developed all the bad habits of imbalance and inattention that adults pick up as they grow older. Adults forget how little they really know. And the more they forget, the further they are from The Way. But young children start out on The Way because everything is new to them. When you start to study any of the martial arts," he held up his hand and began to tick them off on his fingers, "boxing, wrestling, karate, kung fu, tae kwan do, aikido, capoeira, pencak silat, ju jitsu, muy thai, tai chi, arnis, sambo, you have to begin with your mind as open as that of a little child."

"Beginner's mind," I replied.

Uncle John smiled. "Good. You read that in a book

about Zen meditation, didn't you?"

"Unh-hunh."

"Ever try it?"

"*Nda*," I said in Abenaki. "No."

Uncle John held out his right hand and placed it on my brow. As he held it there, it seemed as if his hand got warmer and warmer until it was almost burning. Then he slowly drew his hand away and swung it out in a slow, wide, graceful circle before looking back at me.

I nodded. Whenever Uncle John made one of what he called his "too-long speeches," he would follow it up with silent teaching. His gesture was reminding me, without words, that I had to stop just living in my head. I had to open my mind and my body to the Circle. Knowing a bunch of facts doesn't do much good if you don't under-stand how they connect to the world around us. I lifted my right hand to my brow and then slowly tried to copy that same slow, sweeping gesture.

By our second week together, we had settled into a rou-tine. Each morning I would put in that half hour of train-ing before school, but Saturdays and Sundays were the best. On Saturdays we can keep going until mid-morning when Uncle John has to leave for the part-time weekend mechanic job he found at a local garage. Just enough hours a day to pay for his gym fees and still have enough left over to help us out with the groceries and utility bills. On Sundays we could train together until Mom tells us it's time for us to go to St. Anne's. Uncle John was raised Catholic, just like Mom and me, and we never miss going to church for the late mass.

It was during our second Saturday that Uncle John showed me the hand techniques for the first time. I'd been sort of prepared for learning how to strike. My reading had taught me that *karate* means "way of the fist" in Japanese, just as *tai chi chuan* means "supreme ultimate fist" in Chinese. So I knew I'd be learning punching techniques, ways to fight with my hands and my feet. After all, Uncle John himself was a professional fighter. He thought he had a chance to win that $120,000 challenge and be the "last man standing" in the two-day long War at the Shore, as the upcoming mixed-martial arts tournament had been dubbed by the Koacook Fight Commission.

But, as I was learning, Uncle John didn't do things the way I expected. That second Saturday, after our morning run to the sunrise, a run that we did every day whether it was rainy or dry, warm or bone-chilling cold, he had looked me over as I stood in my usual place next to the picnic table. My feet were shoulder-width apart, my knees a little bent, my back straight, arms loose at my sides, head up. I was relaxed and breathing and, to be honest, a little impatient.

When were we going to get to the punching and kicking that I knew it was all about?

Uncle John cocked his head as he looked at me. "What?" he asked.

It's a trick question, I thought. *He's testing me.* I bit my lip. There had to be some kind of question I could ask him that might lead to the answer I wanted, something that would show him I was ready for the next stage in my training. Then it came to me. After two weeks together, I still didn't know what exact style I was learning. Even though I had read that most martial arts schools begin by teaching you how to count in Japanese or Chinese or Korean or Indonesian, I hadn't been given any consistent vocabulary in an Asian language. Instead, one day he might give me a word in Chinese, another day one in Japanese. But the only language other than English that we used with any regularity was Abenaki. So I was burning with curiosity. I'd been told more than once not to ask, but to observe. But now that Uncle John had actually said "what?" here was an opening. There *was* a way I might find out, a question I *could* use to figure it out on my own.

"What shall I call you?" I asked.

"Hunh?" Uncle John replied.

"I mean, should I call you 'Sensei' or 'Sifu' or, uh, 'Pendetta' or—"

"How about just calling me Uncle John?" Then he laughed. "Cody, I get it. You want to know what style I'm teaching you, right? You think if I answer 'Sifu,' it'll be Chinese. If I answer 'Sensei,' it'll be Japanese? Right?"

I nodded, feeling my face get hot.

Uncle John patted my shoulder. "It's okay," he said. "I was like that, too. But the answer is 'none of the above.' I'm teaching you no style at all. I'm just helping you get your feet started on The Way. Sit."

I let my feet fold under me so that I dropped down—not fast, but controlled—into a sitting position with my legs crossed. It had taken me two whole days to learn how to do that without using my hands or falling to one side.

"Lecture time," Uncle John said, sitting down in front of me. "To begin with, I'm not a master. I know enough to teach you the basics, but I'm only one step on what can be a long road for you. I'm nobody. I'm only a few feet further down the path than you are. Heck, maybe I'm even a few steps behind you. I am far from being worthy of any title of honor."

Uncle John's eyes seemed to cloud then. He rubbed his forehead with his knuckle, a gesture I'd never seen him do before. It was as if he was remembering something that made his head hurt. Then, just like that, he focused on me again. The faraway look left his eyes and was replaced by the hawk-like intensity I'd grown so used to seeing.

"I'm only going to be here for a little while, Nephew. After I'm gone, it'll be your job to find a teacher who can take you further along that path. It might be any one of those arts that you've read about, maybe more than one. But it will all be The Way. Karate, kung fu, it doesn't matter any more than having a black belt really matters in the larger scale of things. And all those paths lead to the same place."

Uncle John placed his left hand on his chest. "Not just a physical and a mental place, but a place of the spirit. The seventh direction. What one of my Lakota buddies when I was in the Corps called 'The Eye of the Heart.' It's a big circle, Cody. It's so big that sometimes you think you're just going in a straight line. Some people don't even see how it's all connected together. But our old people knew, just as they knew that everything is sacred and everything is alive. They learned from the animals, who were out first teachers. Same thing with the first martial artists who became known as masters. You know from your reading about that, don't know? They learned the way of the praying mantis." He held up his hand in the imitation of a mantis claw. "They saw how the tiger moved and struck."

With a fluid motion, he rose up to his feet, leaped in the air to throw a spinning kick followed by a double strike, first to one side and then to the other, with his hands turned into the clawed paws of a great cat before folding himself back down into the relaxed sitting posture he had leapt up from. It had taken only a few effortless seconds for him. But it left me open-mouthed and breathless.

"So," he said, "if anyone asks you what style you're learning, you can just tell them No Style."

Then he rose to his feet, and I mirrored him as he held out his hands in one position after another, and I learned by copying. Open hand. Knife hand. Hammer fist. Crane. Tiger. Snake. . . .

*   *   *   *   *

Uncle John reaches down and feels my calf. I've now been standing here for at least a million years. "Nope." He shakes his head slowly. "What my old tai chi sifu would say about now is," he changed the tone of his voice, "'Too tight. You stay there. I come back in half an hour when you relax.'" Then he chuckles. "Just kidding. You can put your other foot down now. You did fine."

I lower my raised foot as slowly as I can. As soon as I do, the muscle in the leg I've been standing on contracts, and I have to sit down. It's like having hot needles jammed into my calf.

Uncle John goes down on one knee and massages my leg. "Relax," he says. "Let it go into the earth."

Easy for him to say. But the massage works, and the pain

melts away, flowing down in the earth.

Everything goes back into the earth. Back into the Circle. Every leaf that falls feeds the roots of the plants. And in a similar way that both the ancient Chinese and our Abenaki ancestors taught, we can let loose of all our tension, our stress, our pain, and allow the earth to transform it back into balance and health.

Uncle John and I sit together on the earth of our backyard. It may seem like a small space, but it is connected to every other part of the earth. It is only as small as our minds make it seem to be.

Uncle John sighs.

I wait. If I say anything now, it might stop Uncle John from saying what I hope is about to come.

"I guess it's time," Uncle John says, "for me to explain a few things."

Chapter 13

BROKEN MIRRORS

The fool forgets
what he forgot to remember.
—Pendetta Satu

Once again, I sit and wait. Uncle John sits next to me, and I have copied his exact posture: legs crossed as I sit on the ground, back straight, my hands relaxed in my lap, my eyes closed. Breathing deeply in. And out.

I know Uncle John is going to explain "some things" to me. But I also know—now that I've known him for four whole weeks—that he is going to do it in his own time. And his time is Indian Time, not clock time.

People who aren't Skins get confused about what Indian Time really is. Some just think it means that Indians are always going to arrive late. But that's not it at all. It's that many of us remember that "time," in the sense of clocks, is something very new. The oldest, truest form of time is both deeply universal—like the rising and setting of the sun—and as real as the movement of the seasons. True time can't be measured or experienced by clocks because it is also a deeply personal, subjective experience. Have you ever noticed how when you are doing something unpleasant, the time just drags? A minute can seem like hours. But when you are having fun, time seems to fly by. You just got started, and all of a sudden it's over.

Dad told me a story about time, about how our old people came up with a name for the clock. We didn't have clocks before the Platzmoniak, the French people who colonized the northern coast of the Northeast, arrived. But we saw how important their watches and clocks were because they were always looking at them. So we had to make up a word that would describe just what this new ticking thing was that the hairy-faced men in their black robes worshipped as much as they worshipped their wooden statue of a poor, tortured man.

How do they use this new thing? That is what our ancestors asked themselves as they watched the French Jesuits. And they saw that those Europeans used the clocks to tell them when to go to bed and when to get up. Strange, for we just went to bed when it was dark and rose to greet the sun. They used clocks to tell them when to eat. Stranger still. We just ate when we were hungry. Strangest of all, they used those clocks to tell them when to pray. And we prayed whenever we wished to give thanks to Creation, which was often throughout the day.

So the Abenaki word our ancestors came up with for the clock became this: *papulkweezultozik*, which means "that thing which makes much noise but does nothing at all of any real use."

From what I've learned thus far, it seems to me that the ancients who first developed martial arts had an understanding of time like that of my Abenaki ancestors. If you put your mind in the right frame, you can slow things down or make them go quickly. I've even been able to do a little of that myself. Take my bus ride to school as an example. It used to seem like the trip lasted forever. I dreaded it because I always thought that something bad would happen to me whenever I got on that bus.

Not an irrational fear. More like prophetic knowledge. Or a conditioned reflex, like a dog that cringes whenever the person who's abused it comes into the room, even though cringing will probably attract even more abuse.

But once I started to relax and breathe, I stopped cringing. I stopped mentally writing irrational scenarios of the bad things that were about to happen to me that were as much of my fantasy life as those daydreams about being a hero. And the bus ride that used to take forever became bearable most days and hardly even noticed on others.

I couldn't believe how fast things had changed just by my changing my attitude. It's as if one minute I was the target and then, somehow, I was the bow and the arrow.

*   *   *   *   *

I have to admit that not having Grey Cook on the bus for the first two days after Uncle John started teaching me how to relax helped. It gave me time to get used to thinking of myself in different terms, to look into the cloudy mirror and not see a hopeless wimp. Grey didn't show up again until Wednesday of that first week. The bus pulled up, and there he was at his usual window. Instead of looking away from him like I usually did, ducking my head down and hunching up my shoulders, I just kept my focus on the whole bus and kept my back straight, waiting for the door to open. I saw Grey with my peripheral vision, but didn't stare at him.

Grey had been my tormenter ever since I'd started riding that bus in late August. Seeing him had made my stomach feel like it was a washing machine entering the spin cycle. But the funny thing was that by observing him this new way, feeling calm and unafraid, I was actually seeing him more clearly than I had before. I saw, for example, that he had a red bruise on his cheek, and I remembered then how often I'd seen marks like that on his face. Grey wasn't an athlete, so he hadn't gotten those bruises on the football field, like the scrape marks on the faces of the jocks. Where had they come from? And as soon as I asked myself that question, I knew the answer. They'd come from someone in his home. His father.

My parents, even at their worst moments of disagreement, had never hit me. They tried to live by the old teachings of our people. Never strike a child. If he does something wrong, talk to him or tell him a story. Physical abuse can break a child's spirit, twist that child's heart. That's the way all of our people tried to do it in the old days. But I'm old enough and I've seen enough to know it's not that way now. Because of all the pressure of the modern world, because of drinking and all the anger and frustration some Native people carry around with them like a huge burden-basket full of poison, it's not uncommon for Indian kids to be abused by their parents.

And this time, I saw as I got on the bus, it had been even worse for Grey. He didn't just have a bruise on his face; his left arm was in a sling. This day *he* was the one with hunched shoulders and his head down. He didn't let loose a single insult at me or look up at me at all as I got on and took an empty seat.

As more kids got on, the bus filled up. One of them, a sophomore guy whose name I didn't know yet, said "hi" and took the seat next to me again. Since I'd stopped acting like a whipped puppy, the space next to me was no longer being avoided like I had the avian flu. I said "hi" back at him. He probably didn't hear me over the sound of his music. Hip-hop as usual. Kanye West turned up so high I felt the throb of the music.

When we got to school, Hip-hop Kid was slow getting out of his seat. As a result, I was sliding over just as Grey Cook came up behind me. My seat was on the right side, so even though his left arm was in a sling, it was easy for him to swing his other fist hard at the back of my head.

But instead of him hitting me, something else happened. Almost without my telling it to do so, my left hand floated up in that motion I'd been practicing again and again, maybe a thousand times since Uncle John first showed it to me: The Student Offers the Master a Cup of Tea. My circling hand intersected Grey's awkward punch, directing it off to the side and then down. Grey stumbled forward. He might have flipped over the back of the bus seat if I hadn't finished that circle by bringing the palm of my hand up to his shoulder to stop his fall.

"Are you okay?" I asked him, looking into his confused, hurt face and wondering how I ever could have been afraid of him. I waited until he nodded. Then I turned and got off the bus, my steps as calm as my breathing.

In. And *out.*

*   *   *   *   *

Uncle John lets out a deep, strong breath. I do the same, trying to match the length of his, but falling far short. In the Black Tiger breathing he's been showing me, you inhale for a slow count of thirty, hold your breath down in the area around your diaphragm for another count of twenty, then exhale for a second slow count of thirty. In terms of clock time, that means every full breath takes more than a minute. Do sixty of those, and more than an hour has gone by.

"Last night at dinner," Uncle John says, diving straight in, "did you understand what the Tribal Chairman was talking about?"

I shake my head no. I didn't understand much of anything about last night. Why did Mr. Chahna say he'd decided to make an exception in Uncle John's case, in spite of his record? Why did the TC keep calling my mom by her first name? And why was she so friendly with him?

Uncle John looks into my eyes. "I'll let your mother explain her part of it. I'm grateful for her using her influence to speak up for me the way she did."

I nod.

Uncle John looks down into his hands as if they are holding a book he's about to read from. "Started when I was seven," he says. "I was an angry kid. I went to a tough school with kids of all kinds. I hated it when other kids put me down for being Indian. I was always getting into fights. So my adopted parents decided I needed some kind of physical discipline, and they enrolled me in a tae kwon do school.

"My first sensei said I had a gift—at least for the physical and mental parts of it. I soaked it all in like a dry sponge dropped into a pond. I kept on until I had my black belt. Then I took up Kempo. Then capoeira, Northern Shaolin, judo, pencak silat, Brazilian ju-jitsu . . ." He ticks off a long list of names on his fingers, moving from one hand to the other and then back again.

"You could find just about any form of the martial arts you wanted in Los Angeles, and my adopted parents never said no whenever I wanted to try something new. Seven black belts in as many styles. I even joined the wrestling team and won the sectionals at 137 in my freshman year in high school. I had it all together as far as mind and body go. But mental and physical—those are only two parts of the Circle. The spiritual and the emotional sides . . . I couldn't even see them. And I still got angry.

"Every teacher I ever had saw that anger. It got me disqualified in point-sparring tournaments when I'd knock an opponent down when just making light contact was all that was needed. My senseis and sifus all tried to help me find a way to work through my anger and aggression—and none of them succeeded.

"Finally, when I was your age, I thought I'd found the answer. Boxing, where you can hit someone else as hard as you want. Kickboxing first; then Golden Gloves. I was even an Olympic hopeful for a while. But even that wasn't enough for me. I thought I needed more of a challenge. So, as soon as I turned eighteen, I enlisted."

Uncle John takes another slow breath. "I was a good Marine. Made sergeant in record time. And because I was such a good Marine, you know where I ended up? Where every Marine wants to end up—in combat. Afghanistan first. And tough as it was, it felt right to be there, especially after 9/11. I wasn't the only one angry then. What we did there made sense, trying to find Osama bin Laden."

He places his hands on his knees and I wait.

"But after that, it was Iraq. Three tours of duty and each one worse than the one before. I finally learned where anger can take you." He lifts his hands from his lap, turns them over, and looks at his palms. "Cody," he says, "you don't want to go there."

Where? Iraq? The place anger takes you? Then I decide it must be both.

"The first letter I ever got from your mother was during my first tour. I hadn't known I had a sister, and I couldn't believe it at first. But I wrote back to her. And before long, I couldn't believe how much we were alike—except for the fact that she didn't have that burden of anger I'd been carrying around for so long. Your mom, my big sister, is one smart person, Nephew. She helped me realize that all I had to do was put it down.

"But I didn't put that anger down fast enough. One day I got angry at my lieutenant. We were all under a lot of stress, so it's possible that he was in the wrong that day. If I'd just kept my mouth shut, it would have all blown over. But I talked back, and then the next thing I knew, he was down on the ground and I was on top of him. I broke his jaw, and when the other guys in my unit, buddies who'd stood by me, tried to pull me off him, I fought them, too. They say it took a dozen people to finally subdue me, but all I remember is being in the middle of this red cloud of rage. Of course, it ended with me being sent up on charges for striking a superior officer. I was court-martialed and found guilty. I spent three months in the brig—prison. I was on my way to a dishonorable discharge.

"But my lieutenant—the same guy whose jaw I broke—and my buddies spoke up on my behalf. I was under stress. I'd been a good Marine before that. Because they stood by me—even though I didn't deserve it—I was released early from the brig and drummed out of the Corps with just a conditional discharge."

He shakes his head. "Even though they let me out, the

Defense Department still has it all on my permanent record. If you know where to go, you can find the summary of my court-martial and conviction. That's part of what the TC was talking about when he mentioned my record."

Uncle John in prison? Being in the armed forces has always been a tradition in my family, like it is in most Indian families. My dad served and my grampas on both sides. And none of them ever got court-martialed. I'm trying to picture Uncle John as a prisoner, locked up like an eagle in a cage.

But Uncle John starts talking again before I can finish that thought. "That's not the end of my record, though. When I got back stateside, I didn't know what to do with myself. I started drinking. And when I was drunk, I got into trouble. I never hit anyone. I just broke things. Mostly mirrors in bars when I looked in them and didn't like what I saw. So I spent a lot of time in city and county lock-ups on misdemeanor charges. I used up what money I'd saved and started living on the street. A year went by like that. I'd get work washing dishes or repairing engines for a few days, and then I'd have enough to start again. I'd find where the other down-and-out Indians hung out, the street chiefs, you know. Then I'd wake up in the gutter with no memory of how I got there."

He reaches up to pull down his lower lip. "Like the morning in Gallup when I woke up tasting blood and found these two back teeth missing."

My uncle lets out a sigh that comes from someplace even deeper inside him than the breath of the Black Tiger. "Then, one day, I heard a voice. It wasn't DTs. It was my oldest teacher. He wasn't there in the flesh. But it was his voice. Somehow, he was speaking to me. '*Go back to what you know.*' That's what his voice said. And it made me think about what going back really meant. It meant going back to who I really was, to being Indian, as well as to everything I'd learned in twenty years of training. It meant finding The Way."

Uncle John smiles. "I was in the Twin Cities then. I started going to the American Indian House there, talking from my heart. I stopped drinking. I started going to the sweat lodge. And I saw The Way for the first time in my life. It wasn't just the way of the fist; it was the way of the heart. And when I heard the beat of the drum and realized I was listening to my own heart and the heart of the earth and that Mother Earth would always be there for me, I let go of my anger. I accepted who I am."

Uncle John chuckles. "Of course, who I am is a fighter. Fighting is what I know best—sport fighting, not fighting because you're angry at yourself and want to take it out on someone else. Going up against another man who just might beat you in a fair fight if you don't do your best. I knew that was what I wanted to do again. So I started training. I also started writing to your mother again, and she wrote back letters that encouraged me to keep trying. It wasn't easy.

"I tried getting back into boxing, but I couldn't get a license, even in Las Vegas. Plus the business is so tied up with promoters and managers and trainers that you really have to know someone to get in the door. But there were Toughman Contests. After I won enough of those, I moved on to mixed-martial-arts fights. They were being staged mostly in Indian casino arenas in different parts of the country, and being Indian helped me get in. It wasn't the *UFC* on Spike TV, but I was still able to earn some money by winning on the undercard. I matched up fine with anyone they put me against. I wasn't just a striker or just a wrestler, like some of those guys. I had my black belt in Gracie jiu-jitsu, and I'd studied muay thai overseas. I was good on my feet, and I had a better ground game than most. Before long, I'd built up a respectable record."

I looked up for a second at Uncle John's face. I'd noticed the scar tissue around his eyes before, but hadn't thought about how he'd gotten it. Now I knew that it was from punches and kicks and elbow strikes, that his cauliflower ears were from those years of grappling and wrestling; that the bent shape of his nose was from absorbing punishment in the ring.

"I was still homeless," he went on, "but I didn't feel lost anymore. When you're following The Way, and your feet are on Mother Earth, you're never far from home. If you know how to take care of yourself, you don't need much to live. I could hunt and fish and gather plants for food in the country, and when I was in the city, Dumpster diving was the way to go. You'd be amazed at all the good food that gets thrown out behind every restaurant at night. I'd earned enough from my fights that I was able to get good camping equipment. Had enough left over to pay gym fees in whatever town I was doing my training, and even put a little money aside. But I was still hoping for one big break. And when your mom wrote me about the tournament at Koacook Moon, I knew that could be my chance. And here I am."

Uncle John nods and bites his lower lip. He's finished all he has to say, and he's waiting for my response. He's hoping I'll tell him that I can still respect him, even after all I now know about him. But I sit here in silence.

"Nephew?" he asks.

There's too much to absorb. My chest feels tight.

I look over at Uncle John's tent set up in the corner of our backyard. I try to picture it under the pines of a southwestern sky or in an alley where broken beer bottles crunch underfoot. How can I picture this strong, tall man as a convicted prisoner who attacked his own buddies in wartime or as a street chief, a hopeless drunk feeling sorry for himself? I know there aren't easy answers for everything in life, but right now I'm not even sure what the right questions are.

I'm no longer sitting. I don't remember getting up, but I am standing in front of him. My hands are clenched into fists as if I'm about to fight someone.

"I gotta go," I mumble. I turn and thrust my way through the gate so hard that it falls halfway off its hinges and jams open.

And even though a part of me wants my uncle to come running after me, another part is glad when I look over my shoulder and see him still sitting there, studying his hands again.

Chapter 14

AND PEOPLE CHANGE

The broken egg
cannot grow a new shell.
—Sensei Ni

I'm running angry. My heavy feet aren't gliding over the ground. They are slapping down hard on the pavement as if I'm trying to break the concrete. My chest is burning, and I know I'm breathing all wrong. But I keep thudding along, punishing myself with every step. I get to where the trail into the woods begins, and even though I don't intend to take it, I find myself swerving off into the forest, and the thudding concrete is replaced by the soft cushion of generations of pine needles.

The ground absorbs my anger and confusion as I run, and my steps grow lighter, my breath comes more even. I don't feel like a robot with stiff limbs as I climb the hill where the light is growing stronger.

The sun is about to come up. I should head back home or I'll miss the bus. I don't care. I'm never going home again. Or back to school. I'm going to sit here on this hillside until I sink into the ground.

I ease myself into a cross-legged position, relax my arms, and straighten my back. I breathe in the cool autumn air and the warm sunlight. In. And out. My heart slows down, and so do the thoughts that have been twisting inside my head. Nothing is perfect in this world. You can never find even one leaf without a single blemish. But when you put everything together, it all connects. It makes a circle.

I breathe in and out. In. Hold. And out. Slowly. Twenty times. Twenty minutes. Then I get up and start walking back. At one point the trail comes close to an overhang near the highway. I can hear the humming roar of early-morning traffic below, and if I part the branches, I can see the road below. I lean against the rough bark of a pine and look.

Sure enough, there goes my bus without me. And there, halfway back, is Grey Cook. He's wearing the same brown flak jacket he showed up in two weeks ago. He's holding a phone up, and the way he's tapping it, I can tell that he's text-messaging someone. I wonder what he's texting this early.

He's probably sending something strange like what I

saw on his phone the other day when he dropped it getting off the bus. His phone didn't hit the floor because I caught it in mid-air and handed it to him. No "thank you" from him. He no longer even makes eye contact with me. He just took the phone and clutched it to his chest. But I'd already seen the message:

r u there

i m heer

i m rtk

r u rtk

I wonder who he's messaging. The breakdown into groups in our school isn't really racial. It doesn't matter if you are Indian or white. What's important is how you look, what you do, what music turns you on. Sure, there's a bunch of what they call the Super-Indians, kids who wear lots of native jewelry and let their hair grow long and straight if they are girls or have their hair cut into a Mohawk if they are guys. But there are Indian kids who are preppies and jocks and gangsters (as in gangster rap), even some who are goths. Grey, though, doesn't hang with any of them.

After I stopped being afraid of him, I began to realize that he was sort of a misfit, too. He always sits alone on our bus. It was like the only relationship he'd had in school was with me—him as persecutor and me as victim. Weird. Seeing him from this distance, for the first time I notice how much he reminds me of someone else now—maybe not in his facial features and his shape so much as the vibe around him, like the dark ink cloud of a squid. Jackson Teeter. Stump. And I remember seeing the two of them together. Double weird.

I breathe in and out one more time, then get up and head back down the hill. Now that I've had time to think about them, Uncle John's words make sense to me. I'm no longer confused about him. Everyone makes mistakes. Especially me. But people can change.

As I get close to our trailer, I see that the gate in the backyard fence has been put back on its hinges. I was ready to do that, but Uncle John has beat me to it. He's nowhere to be seen. Probably off on his own run now. I'll talk to him later and tell him that it's okay. I'm cool with it.

Mom's car is out front. That's good. I can ask her to write me a note and then take me in to school. If I'm lucky, I'll only miss my first period, and I won't get detention for being late.

"Are you okay, honey?"

Those are Mom's first words, even before I can say "good morning" to her.

I start to answer that I'm fine, but I don't. I sit down across from her and put my hands flat on the red plastic tablecloth.

"Mom, I'm confused."

"About Uncle John?"

I shake my head. "No, I think I understand. I mean about you. What's going on?"

"What do you mean?" Mom's voice is nervous. I'm not used to that. Loving, concerned, tired, even resigned. But not nervous.

"You're looking happier lately, and you're dressing nicer. And how come Mr. Chahna was so friendly with you at dinner? What was up with that?"

She purses her lips, then reaches up to twist the strand of hair that has fallen in front of her eye.

"Cody," she says, "your father isn't . . ." She bites her lip, unable to say the rest of it.

And that's when it hits me. I realize what a dope I've been not to see it. Because I haven't wanted to see it.

"Dad's not coming back, is he?"

For a moment Mom closes her eyes. Then she takes a breath, a shallow one, reaches out and puts her hands on top of mine. She doesn't have to say anything. I know. The answer is no.

"Why?" I have to ask, even though I don't want to know. Part of me wants to keep pretending that the next thing we'll hear is the deep, throbbing engine of his truck as it pulls up in front, and then he'll be coming through the door with a big smile and his arms spread wide to embrace us both.

"Some things just can't be fixed after they're broken, Cody. And people change." Her hands tighten on mine. "He'll always be your father. He loves you. And he wants you to visit him whenever you can. But he's not coming back. His life is going one way and mine is . . ." Her voice trails off.

We just sit here like this. I could say that we're sitting together in silence, but it's not silent. The cheap, battery-run clock on the wall is ticking so loud that it sounds like one of those corny movie countdowns to doom. The compressor in the refrigerator is humming louder and louder like some crazy hive of mutant bees. The heat of the sun is making the trailer itself give off these unearthly creaking and cracking sounds as the metal on the outside expands. Both Mom and I are aware of the growing noise around us. From her one raised eyebrow, I can tell that it's striking her the way it is me. Here we are in the midst of a family melo-drama, and all we can hear are these cartoon sounds around us.

TICK-TOCK-TICK-TOCK
WHHHRRRRR
WHA-DONK!
This final breathless moan from the metal sheath of our

pathetic home is just too much. We look up at each other, and we can't help it. We both start laughing and don't stop until we have tears in our eyes.

I squeeze Mom's hands and then let go of them.

"I'm really late for school," I say.

"Okay," Mom answers, picking up her car keys. "I'm ready to get going. Okay?"

"Yeah, I'm ready, too."

Chapter 15

UP THE HILL

Speak with your mouth shut.
See with your eyes closed.
—Sifu Sahn

Mr. Randall looks out at the faces of twenty teenagers who are still dazed from having to get up before dawn. Or are mesmerized by whatever downloaded tunes are running into their ears, making them mindless bobbleheads.

"Unplug," Mr. Randall says.

Most of the kids actually do. A measure of the respect he enjoys—unlike some other teachers. It was just his bad luck this term to have his Survey of Modern World History slotted into second period. Randall, who used to be a pro baseball player, is not a bad guy. He doesn't talk at you like some teachers do. Or nod as if his worst expectations were being confirmed when someone makes a dumb response. He tries to talk to you and work with you to help you understand. Today his theme is world peace, about whether or not we need to change our approach from armed conflict to mediation. Despite my bad mood, I find myself really listening to his words.

"So," he says, spreading his hands out toward us, "who thinks that the United Nations is a modern version of the Greek myth of Sisyphus?"

Lots of blank looks.

"Okay, I'll back up. Who knows who Sisyphus was?"

No one raises a hand. Either they haven't got a clue, or they'd rather not put themselves on the spot. Or, like me, they feel as if they're the ones condemned to push that huge boulder up the hill, lose control of it just when they are about to reach the top, and watch it roll all the way back to the bottom again.

It's a familiar feeling for me. Even if, for the last few weeks, that feeling of hopelessness had been fading, it has returned like the Terminator. It's as if I've taken a giant step backwards after weeks of edging slowly forward an inch at a time.

Mr. Randall's wall phone rings.

"Hold that thought," he says to us before he answers it.

Aside from the sound of stray beats bleeding out of unplugged iPods, it is so quiet in the class that I can hear the humming of the banks of fluorescent lights overhead.

Mr. Randall is up front holding the wall phone to his ear. He's not saying anything, just nodding.

I look up at the clock on the wall. I could care less if it froze there forever or if its hands spun like a top. It doesn't matter either way. I've got nowhere to go; nowhere I want to be. Nothing makes sense. Not my training, not my mother or my father or my life. Yeah, I was laughing with Mom when I left this morning, but as we drove to school, it hit me.

Dad's not ever coming home. We're not a family anymore.

By the time I got out of the car, I felt as if my stomach was full of sand. I'm angry at them, and I'm angry at me. Although, maybe it's all my fault. What did I do to make all this happen? If I'd been a better son, would my mom and dad still be together? There must have been something more I could have done. *I am such a loser.* I bite my tongue to keep from shouting those words out loud.

And then it happens. Something Uncle John said speaks itself in my mind in a clam, clear voice.

"Just because everything is connected does not mean you are responsible for everything that happens."

I didn't understand that when he first said it a month ago. And right now I don't want to understand it. I don't want to understand that I can't change everything in the world and make it better.

"Okay," Uncle John's voice continues. "How about this? The Serenity Prayer.

> 'Lord, grant me the patience
> to accept the things I cannot change,
> the courage to change the things I can,
> and the wisdom to know the difference.'"

Oh shut up, I think. But there's a little smile coming to my face in spite of it. What a self-pitying jerk I've been! And when did God step aside and tell me I was responsible for everything that happens in the world?

I feel the clouds lifting from around my head. Things may not be the way I want them to be. But how bad off am I? Really?

All I have to do is look around me at some of the other kids in my class. They have better clothes and electronic stuff, but I know that none of them have parents who love them more than my mom and dad love me, even if they aren't together. Some kids have only one parent, and even that one parent treats them like they are dogs.

I look over my shoulder to the desk where Jackson Teeter is supposed to be sitting. Just as in first period, we have our second class of the day together. Except he isn't here. Which is the second weird thing today that has to do with him.

The first had been when I saw him in the hall after I gave the office secretary the note from my mom explaining my lateness. Since I am maybe the only kid in school aside from Grey Cook who ever notices that Stump is alive, I was surprised when he didn't nod back to me. Instead he avoided eye contact, shifted his bigger-than-usual black backpack (but with the same "LIFE SUCKS" motto printed on it in Wite-Out) and slouched around the corner ahead of me. I was headed in the same direction to our second period class, only about twenty feet behind him, but when I turned the corner, there was no sign of him. It was like he had vanished. That was Weird Thing Number One.

The bell rings, ending second period. I'm better . . . which means I'm not feeling like Atlas, another victim of the penal system of the Greek gods. So when I am about to pass Mr. Randall, still stuck on the phone, I stop.

"Cruel king of Corinth," I say. "Punishment in Hades was to spend eternity pushing a heavy stone up a hill only to have it constantly roll down again."

Mr. Randall's face lights up like a hundred-watt bulb. He presses the mouthpiece of the phone against his shoulder. "One for the home team," he says with a grin, giving me a big thumbs-up. Then he holds up a right hand the size of a catcher's mitt for me to slap him five.

I'm smiling, too, as I step out into the hall. It's amazing

how doing something that makes another person feel good can do the same for you.

Someone shoves me from behind. Five weeks ago I would have fallen on my face. But this time I just take a little step to the side and pivot so the person shoving me goes off-balance and stumbles past me. He quickly catches his balance and turns to loom over me. It's Jeff Chahna.

"You jerk!" he says, spitting his words at me.

What have I done to him? Aside from bruising his knuckles on my nose, that is? I just look at him. He's bigger than me, but I'm not feeling scared. Or hostile. And because of that, the look on his face changes from anger to confusion. I read his body language, the hand bunched into a fist, the open mouth. He wants to say something, but he doesn't know how to say it.

"You don't belong here," he finally blurts out.

I can believe that. But I also know that's not what he really means. I realize that now I know what's making him angry—because it's part of what made me angry. My mom and his dad. At that dinner, Mr. Chahna made it pretty plain that he was hoping my mom would agree to go out with him. He'd mentioned twice that it had been a year and a half since his divorce was final. And both times Jeff had looked like he was trying to swallow a rock.

I hold up both of my hands, open, palms out. What can I do?

Jeff glares at me, then pushes past. I step back to avoid being clobbered by his big backpack.

But not as big as the one Stump had today.

You aren't supposed to run in the halls, so I start walking as fast as I can. I think I know where Stump disappeared to, and I've got a sick feeling in my stomach.

I hope I'm wrong.

Chapter 16

INSIDE

The eyes see more
and less than the mirror.
—Master Net

They give us seven minutes to get from one class to the next. That's better than a lot of schools I've been in. It makes things a little less hectic and hurried in the halls. In the junior high school I was at a year ago, they gave us only three minutes, and the result was a frenzied mob of pre-teens swarming like lemmings looking desperately for the nearest tall cliff.

During Long River's grace period, some kids just saunter along, cell phones to their ears, checking out each other's clothes or breaking up into little cliques to compare the music in their iPods.

I'm not doing any of those things. All I can see is Stump being humiliated that day outside the library. It wasn't at this time of the day, between second and third period. It was later, just before lunch. So maybe I still have time.

Or maybe I am just imagining it. Maybe I'm back to creating one of those scenes in which I become the hero. I shake my head. No.

"What would you do," asked Uncle John after teaching me about The Way one morning, "if you found yourself in Central Park in New York City at midnight surrounded by four muggers with knives?"

I thought hard before answering that one. I'd learned enough to know that fantasizing I could actually beat four armed men in a fight was foolish. That was what the old Cody would have imagined. None of that kicking the knife out of one man's hand, side-kicking the second, spinning leg sweep on the third, and a knockout punch to the fourth, all in the blink of an eye. That only happens in movies.

"Try talking to them?" I had suggested.

"They won't listen to you," Uncle John said.

I thought again. "Run?"

"They're faster than you. And one of them also has a gun."

Then I got it. "What I would do is not go into Central Park alone at midnight."

"Right," Uncle John said.

So I am headed where any sane kid should head right

now, straight to the A.P.'s office to tell him about what I'm afraid is about to happen. Except, as I make the turn that connects the long, long hallway to the front office, I realize I am going to go right past where I saw Stump disappear first thing this morning. Where could he have gone?

Then a thought comes to me. Something Uncle John told me. *Don't just see what you expect to see. See what is really there.*

I detour around a wheeled green dumpster half full of broken sheetrock and other construction debris from the renovations being done on the boys' locker room. Turn left and there it is. The place where he must have ducked in.

The sign on the door: "Janitor's Closet."

I pause in front of the door and lean back against it as other kids walk past me. The crowds in the hall are thinning out now. Only a minute or two until the bell. I lean my head back and listen. But I don't hear any whispered voices coming from inside the closet. My intuition tells me that no one is in there. Still looking straight ahead, I put one hand behind me and try the doorknob. It should be locked, but the knob turns easily in my hand, and I hear the *click* of the latch as it releases. The door moves in half an inch.

The hall is empty now, so I turn and push the door open. The light is on in the closet, and there's no one hiding inside it. Just the usual stuff you'd expect. A big, wide push mop with a long, red handle. Shelves of paper towels and toilet paper. Industrial-size cans of soap and disinfectant. And a large, black canvas bag wedged into a corner, half-hidden behind a box of paper towels. I wouldn't have noticed it if I hadn't seen the white-lettered word on its side. "LIFE." The hair stands up on the back of my neck.

I look back over my shoulder. Still no one in sight. But I'm sure someone will come down this hallway any minute. I duck into the closet and shut the door behind me.

Somehow I know there's not much time. The first thing I do is to turn the toggle in the middle of the doorknob to lock it from the inside. Which will work fine unless someone has a key. But this closet isn't that deep, just deep enough for the door to have room to swing inward. I grab the long-handled dust mop, wedge its head against the bottom of the door, and press the handle down so that its end is crammed back against the bottom of one of the back shelves. Then I sit down on top of the handle to hold it in place, my back against the door.

Just then, someone jiggles the doorknob next to my ear and then curses.

"It's locked," a voice hisses.

"I've got the key," another voice answers. "Remember? My stupid father has keys that will open any lock."

I hear the jangle of a keychain, the scratch of a key being inserted. The toggle in the middle of the knob and the latch both release.

"All right!" one of the voices says in triumph. I recognize that voice. Grey Cook.

"Not so loud," Jackson Teeter's voice hisses back at him.

I feel the push of a body against the door. But my own weight and the wedged mop hold. The door doesn't open, even when someone's fleshy shoulder thuds hard against it.

A string of expletives comes from the two boys. They're both hurling themselves against the door. But the mop handle is made of fiberglass, and it doesn't even bend. No way are they getting in here.

"Some bloody thing must have fallen down in front of the door and jammed it," Stump growls.

"Man," Grey Cook whimpers, "it's all in there. What are we gonna do?" The tone of his voice has changed. "Maybe it wasn't a good idea. Maybe we should just—"

"Shadow!" Stump hisses. "RTK, remember."

"Jackson, I—"

"There's no Jackson here. Use my real name, my final name. You are Shadow, my brother, and I am . . ."

"Night," Grey says, his voice shaking a little. "But what about all our . . . stuff. How are we going to . . . to take care of things?"

I hear a hand slap against something solid. "We got enough right here. Plus there's the piece I hid in the crapper where we're going to wait until Zero Hour. Right?"

"Right . . . okay."

"RTK?"

Grey pauses.

Don't say it, I think. *Tell him it's a crazy idea. Stop this whole thing.*

But instead, Grey gives a heavy sigh.

"RTK," he says.

I hear the sound of their feet on the tile floor as they move away. Despite their new ninja names, neither of them has learned to walk quietly. I want to jump up, burst out of here, and run. But I know I have to wait to make absolutely sure they're gone.

Plus I have to know.

I crawl over to the corner and pull out the bag that was half-hidden there. Heavy objects shift inside it, and there's the sound of metal hitting metal. I unzip it and look inside. I see the glint of metal and read the word "Mossberg."

Jackson Teeter had taken more from his security guard father's office than that ring of skeleton keys. There are two Mossberg shotguns, three .45 caliber handguns, and at least ten boxes of ammunition, as well as half a dozen deadly souvenirs that his father must have smuggled back into the

127

country after his time in the National Guard in the Middle East. Live hand grenades.

A chill runs down my back. I just figured out the meaning of RTK.

Ready to Kill.

Chapter 17

TIME TO RUN

The hero runs into the fire.
The wise man picks up a water bucket.
—Pendetta Satu

I know I have to do something.

Breathe, I tell myself. *In. And out. Then do the first thing you know is the right thing to do—keep Stump and Grey from getting this bag of weapons.*

I open the closet door and look outside in both directions. I sling the heavy bag over my shoulder and leave the closet, heading away from the direction I heard the two go.

I turn the corner, and there it is. The green dumpster hasn't been moved. I put the bag down, open the lid, and look inside. It seems full, but things have just been thrown in haphazardly. I can make room.

I shift a big piece of sheetrock to one side and push things around with my right hand. And all the time I'm doing this, I keep looking back over my shoulder. Finally there's enough room.

I pick the bag up, lever it over the edge, and let it drop into the bottom of the dumpster. I pull plastic bags and pieces of sheetrock over it until it is completely concealed. I close the lid quietly. And as I dust my hands off, I tell myself to stop holding my breath. Look around.

While I've been doing this, my mind has been mapping out the quickest, safest route to get to the front office—a route that won't take me anywhere near where Stump and Grey have gone. The boys' bathroom is just down the hall from the library, within sight of the place where Stump was pantsed and videoed. I can't take a chance on running into them, having them stop me—or shoot me. I don't want to spook them into putting their plan into action early.

I grab the handle of the dumpster, and the palm of my right hand starts to sting as soon as I do. I must have cut myself moving the junk. No time to stop now, though. I push against the dumpster. Its wheels creak, but it moves. I shove it ahead of me down the short hall. It pushes the two side doors open, bumps over the threshold of the door, but doesn't stop. The light from the bright autumn day almost blinds me. A gray squirrel that had been rummaging around in some leaves piled up against the side of the building skitters away from me and the green metal monster.

I hear the doors click shut behind me. Me and the dumpster and its deadly cargo are now locked out. I still push the dumpster another twenty feet until I can shove it into a little alcove out of sight from inside the building. It'll be safe here, for sure.

I let go of the handle and see the red smear on the green metal. I look at my right palm. Blood is starting to well out of a long line across it. It's starting to throb, a sign that it's a deep wound. I shake my head. I don't have time to worry about that now. I untuck my shirt and tear a strip of cloth off the bottom of it, wrap it around my hand, and use my teeth and my other hand to knot it.

When it's time to run, run fast.

I take off as if I'd just heard a starter's gun. It's a long way around to the front door, especially because my route is going to circle the long way around the right half of the building complex. Stump and Grey were headed in the direction of the left block where the labs and gyms and assembly hall and library are located.

I sprint past classroom windows and see with my peripheral vision that everything is going on as if it is a normal day, except that teachers and students are staring at me as I dash by.

That kid is going to be in deep trouble, they're thinking.

Then I'm at the fence. I jump, hitting it with my hands

131

and feet, climbing, and I finally roll over the top. My shirt catches on something that scratches my chest. When I thrust my body forward, I feel a tug and hear fabric tearing. Then I'm free, somersaulting down to thud onto the hard earth on the other side.

I'm shaking as I get up. The dull ache in my hand is worse, and the strip of blue cloth wound around it has turned a glistening crimson color. I lean against the fence and take a deep breath, forcing the air back into my lungs. In. And out. I'm okay. All the running I've been doing every morning has prepared me for this. I take one step and then another. The weakness I felt in my knees leaves me. I cross the edge of the football field, cut through the end zone, the sacred soil of victory that a wimp like me is never supposed to touch, then I'm on the walkway that leads back around the main building. I turn the corner and see the front steps ahead of me.

The wind moves the flag overhead, and the rope clang-clang-clangs against the metal flagpole. Everything is normal. For a moment, I wonder if I've just been imagining things. I grab the door to pull it open. The throb of pain from my right palm as the locked door doesn't budge reminds me just how real this all is. I hit the button to the right of the doors.

No response.

I press it again, then hold it down, hearing the distant buzzing from inside the locked double doors.

"Yes?" an irritated voice answers through the intercom.

"I'm Cody LeBeau. I'm a freshman."

A pause. No clicking sound of the door being unlocked.

"Why are you outside the school, Mr. LeBeau?"

There's no time for long, crazy-sounding explanations. I have to keep it simple.

"I've got to see the assistant principal. Mr. Mennis."

The door locks click immediately. I push through. There's no one sitting at the desk in front of the doors where Officer Hal usually sits. He's the bored uniformed policeman who's assigned to our lobby on weekday mornings, just like it is now in most of the schools since Columbine and Pearl and Red Lake and all the others. Since he works out at the gym with Uncle John, I've gotten to know Officer Hal. He's probably off getting coffee. Long River's not a place where anyone would expect serious violence.

I sprint forward toward the A.P.'s office fifty feet down the hall to the left. Someone yells, "Hey!" behind me, but I don't look around. My right hand is so bloody now that it slips off the doorknob. I can't turn it. I bang on the door with my fist. The door opens inward. Mr. Mennis's huge shape looms over me like an angry bear.

"What in blue blazes—" he starts. "Son," he says, "you're a bloody mess."

"Two kids," I say, taking a deep breath. I have to stop panting and get my words out clearly. "They're got guns."

Mr. Mennis moves quicker than you'd expect from a man of his size. He pulls me into the office and snatches up the microphone from the speaker system beside his desk.

"Red," he barks into the mike. "I repeat. Red. Red. Red."

Chapter 18

LOCKDOWN

Words run faster than
the swiftest horses.
—Sensei Ni

It turns out that Long River High School is better prepared for the serious threat of school violence than I'd
realized. As soon as Mr. Mennis barks the code word "red"
into the mike, things happen fast.

Administrative assistants pick up telephones to contact
the state and local police. I can hear doors slamming shut
down the halls, even before Mr. Mennis adds the words,
"Lockdown, secure your classrooms" to his urgent message.

Somehow I've missed the lockdown drill those words
probably call for here at Long River, but I know what it was
like at the junior high I attended just outside Chicago 3TPA.
The teacher immediately goes to the door of the classroom,
shuts it, and turns the bolt lock. If there's a window in the

door, every person in the classroom is told to move to the back of the room and to the side. That way anyone who might look in will see only an empty class. I remember this one sixth-grade math teacher who even went so far during those drills as to have the bigger boys in the class help her push her desk across the room to shove it against the door.

Just like a fire drill, except this time everyone is told to stay in rather than to go out. People milling around in the halls, even for the brief time it takes to exit the building, make great targets. The whole idea of an exercise like this is to make sure that people don't make themselves into targets.

Things get quiet fast. It's not just because you have been told to be quiet. It's a silence that descends like a dark blanket falling from the ceiling. Even if you don't believe it's for real, some part of you is listening for the sound that I'm afraid I may hear at any minute—the boom of a shotgun blast or the rapid tat-tat-tat of an automatic weapon.

I listen for the sound of police sirens, even though I don't really expect to hear any yet. In real life, actual emergency response time is never in seconds, but in minutes.

Mr. Mennis puts down the mike and turns back toward me with a questioning look on his face that is just this side of tsunami-scale anger. He's broadcasted the alert, but is the whole thing for real?

"Mr. LeBeau," he growls, "stand up."

He runs his hands over my body, checking to see if I have any weapons. For all he knows—despite my appearance—it might be a trick. He probably suspects me.

He grabs my left arm, probably harder than he means to. That's when I realize that I hurt myself more than I thought. My whole left arm is just limp. When the A.P. grabs it, I hear a clicking sound in my shoulder. I gasp in pain. I think I broke my collarbone when I fell going over the fence. And that explains why I had such a hard time opening the door of his office with my right hand.

I can tell by the look on the A.P.'s face that he heard the sound from my shoulder, too. He quickly lets go of my arm and lifts his hand up, palm toward me in a gesture of apology.

"Son," he says. 'I'm sorry. I just have to know."

I feel like I'm going to be sick. I swallow hard. "It's not a joke."

I take another breath. I can feel sweat forming on my forehead. If I'm going to say anything, I'd better get it out quick because the room is about to pull loose like a tent being hit by a high wind. It'll start spinning any second now.

"There's two of them. Stump—Jackson Teeter, I mean. And Grey Cook. Don't know what they've got. Found most of their stuff. Guns. Hand grenades. Black bag. Hid it . . .

137

bottom of green dumpster . . . north door of the school. Pushed it outside so they couldn't . . . get it."

I'm having trouble with my words. Mr. Mennis's face is next to mine. He's holding me up with one hand on my chest and pressing a towel against my right hand.

The round face of Officer Hal is peering down at me over the A.P.'s broad shoulder. And there's the school nurse. I didn't even hear either of them come into the room. I'm disappointed in myself. After all of Uncle John's training. Letting little things like a broken collarbone and the loss of half of the blood in my body prevent me from paying attention to what's happening around me. Nobody should be able to sneak up on an apprentice ninja.

But my ears are still working, because now I can hear the sound of sirens getting closer. They are the perfect sound effect to go with the merry-go-round that the room and everything and everyone in it have now become.

It would be easy to close my eyes right now, but there's one more thing I have to say, even if it's just a whisper.

"They're in . . . the boys' room by the librar—"

And then the merry-go-round becomes a funhouse tunnel, and I go sliding down into the darkness.

Chapter 19

RED STRIPES

Looking hard for enemies,

you may find yourself.

—Sifu Sahn

My dad told me the story of how our men came to put red paint on their faces when they went off to battle.

Long ago, he said, there was a monster bear that threatened the people of a certain village. No one knew what to do because that bear was so powerful and it was also so stealthy. It would strike without warning and then disappear back into the forest, carrying the body of its victim with it.

One boy, though, was a keen observer and also a great listener. He figured out the pattern of the bear's attacks. He made prayers to the Creator, giving thanks for the gifts of courage and clear thought. Then he went out alone to confront the monster before it could attack his people again.

He was ready to sacrifice himself for his family, if it came to that. He knew that was the right way. He was ready to follow The Way.

Sure enough, just as he had thought, the monster bear came down the trail where the boy was waiting. He heard the bear coming and leaped out to intercept it. The two of them fought. It was a long, hard battle. After using up his arrows and his spears, finally the boy had only his knife left as the great bear closed in on him.

Even though he was just a child, that boy somehow managed to kill the monster bear. Because he was fighting to defend his people, his strength was great. But in his battle with the monster, the boy was wounded. He came back into the village to tell the people that their enemy was dead. They all saw the bloody lines on his cheeks where they had been raked by the sharp claws of the bear.

From then on, whenever men went out to fight in defense of their people, they painted their cheeks with parallel red stripes, like those claw marks made by the monster bear. They did so to honor that boy's courage and to remind themselves that they were fighting for others.

I've never painted my face.

But as they waited in the boys' bathroom near the library, Grey Cook and Jackson Teeter had painted theirs. Not to honor the courage of that long-ago boy, though.

Their motives were rage and personal revenge.

"They called it their war paint," Mom says. "That's what Grey Cook told the police, at least. He said it stood for the blood of all the people they were going to kill."

As I sit here in the hospital bed with my arm in a sling, I listen quietly as my mom and Uncle John tell me about what happened after I blacked out. Officer Hal has filled in my uncle on everything that happened—including the details that probably won't make the news.

"That Cook boy is a sad young man," Uncle John says. "The only thing he ended up shooting off was his mouth. Once they got hold of him, he couldn't stop talking. He never pulled the trigger once, thank the Creator! As soon as he heard the sirens, he panicked, threw the gun out the window, and ran for it. The police officers tackled him in the hallway when he came running out of the bathroom door."

He was scared even before then, I think, remembering how Grey's voice had sounded from the other side of the closet door. If Stump hadn't pushed him, none of it would ever have happened.

"He didn't shoot anyone," Mom continues, "but the other boy did."

Who had Stump shot?

"His father," Uncle John says. "They'd agreed that they'd both kill their fathers first, but the Teeter boy was the only one who tried to go through with it. Three times with a .22 target pistol. But it's not that hard to survive a small-caliber round if it doesn't hit a vital organ."

Uncle John's gaze goes far away for a moment and his right hand starts to drop down toward his left side before he catches himself and puts his hand back onto my good shoulder.

"Even though he was left for dead, Mr. Teeter is going to live," Mom continued. "Not that he deserves to if he did all the things to his son that the boy says he did in that little brown notebook he had on him."

"He wrote it all down," Uncle John adds. "All the names of everyone who mistreated him, and he described the things they had done to him. It was a long list, dozens of names, all under the heading 'KILL FIRST.' Then there were subheadings. 'Teachers,' 'football players,' 'super-Indians,' 'cheerleaders,' 'smart kids,' 'skaters,' 'preppies,' 'pretty girls'—pretty much every group in the school, I'd bet." My uncle shakes his head. "The last name on that list it was his own. He really was at war with the whole world."

I know he's thinking, as I am, about the things that must have happened to Stump to fill him with so much hate for everyone and everything, himself included.

My uncle puts his hand on my chest.

"You know, Cody, Hal told me that your name was in

it, too. But it was in the back of the book where he had a separate list. A very short one with the heading 'DO NOT KILL.'"

"It's a good thing you kept them from those other weapons," Mom says. "Those hand grenades alone . . ."

Uncle John nods. "As it was, all they had left were just two small-caliber target pistols, and the other thing that the Teeter boy apparently had been carrying around with him at school for the last two months. No one even knew he had it."

The image of a fat, mistreated kid dressed in black and huddling alone inside a bathroom stall comes to me. It made me so sad, fills my heart with such pity that I can barely ask the question.

"What happened to Stump?"

Mom bites her lip and then squeezes my hand, forgetting, I guess, that it has over forty stitches in it. I try not to wince.

"When the police tactical squad realized he was alone in the bathroom, they decided to wait him out, especially after he started firing that .22. He wasn't shooting it at anyone. He was shooting out the mirrors."

"The Cook boy told them that Teeter only had the one gun," Uncle John says. "So they waited until the shooting stopped."

My mom and my uncle are still talking, but I'm no longer only hearing their voices. I'm seeing the events unfold in my mind's eye, as if I am an invisible observer.

The bathroom door is propped open and you can see inside. The broken glass from the mirrors is everywhere, reflecting shattered images. You can't see Stump, but from the spent shell casings near the last stall, you can guess that's where he's taken refuge.

"No one's going to hurt you, son," the negotiator on the Tac Squad calls in to Stump.

"Hah!" Stump laughs. "You're a little late for that." His voice sounds both hurt and defiant.

"Just throw out the gun."

There's a long, tense silence. Then a hand reaches out from behind that last stall and flings a gun that comes skittering across the floor toward them. An empty .22 Ruger.

"That's good, son. That's the right thing to do. Now come on out with your hands where we can see them."

What answers them this time is a broken sob.

"I can't get up. I hurt myself. I'm really hurt. You've got to help me."

The men in their flak jackets exchange glances. The false bravado is gone from the boy's voice. He sounds like nothing more than a confused, scared child.

The head of the team stands up and motions for the others

to follow him, guns ready. They move slowly, heavy-booted feet crunching the shards of mirrors. Half a dozen men in black, the adrenaline pumping through their bodies, making them tense as coiled springs. And they also feel a little foolish as they creep forward. It's only a little Indian kid, for cramp's sake. He's only what, fourteen years old?

When they reach the last stall, they look inside. The boy is sitting there, waiting. His brown, chubby face looks almost like that of a clown, marked with thick, wavy, red lines.

His hands are behind his back.

"What took you so long?" the boy asks. Then his face twists into a sickly grin. "Thanks for the help, suckers."

He holds out his hands, palms up. A grenade is balanced on one. The other holds the pin he's just pulled.

Chapter 20

TWO FINGERS TO THE SKY

Knowledge holds power.

Wisdom lets go of it.

—Master Net

"And in this corner-r-r-r," the announcer's voice echoes over the packed crowd, "John Fighting Bear A-wa-ssos-s-s-s-s-s."

Mom turns to me. She's trying not to show how nervous she is, but even though her smile seems relaxed, her tension shows in how hard she squeezes my hand. "At least they pronounced your uncle's name right this time," she says.

They should, I think.

After all, this is the fourth time he's been introduced in the tournament. And he's in the final match of the day after having beaten his first three opponents. If the announcer and the excited throng of people in the sold-out Koacook Moon Casino arena didn't know who he was before the start of the War at the Shore, they sure know him now!

My uncle bows to each of the four directions and then raises his right hand, just as he has done each time he's been introduced, two fingers pointed to the sky. He makes a little circle with his hand, then drops it to tap those two fingers against his chest.

Then he turns and sweeps his hand out in an open-palm gesture that ends at Mom and me where we sit at ringside. A spotlight shines down from the array of lights above the octagon, and I can see that at least one of the TV cameras has been pointed at the two of us. I lift my still-bandaged right hand, tap my own heart, and give a peace sign to the camera.

I'm kind of used to cameras now—or at least I don't let them bother me the way they did during my first interview. I suppose some people watching on TV at home might even still remember who I am, even if it was four weeks ago—which is like four hundred years in news time. When I was in the hospital, I was being visited by a different news crew every hour. But that only went on for a little while.

I was glad for that. Even though lots of kids think that being famous is the greatest thing in the world, I'd learned

147

fast just how intrusive it can be to have your name and your story beamed to the world. Especially when all I wanted to do was get some sleep.

"Thank God for the twenty-four-hour news cycle," Mom said when not a single media vulture showed up two days after the words "TEENAGER AVERTS SCHOOL MAS-SACRE" started crawling across the bottom of cable news broadcasts.

The media blitz would probably have lasted longer if anyone had died. But Jackson Teeter's dad is recovering from his gunshot wounds. And even though the tactical squad dove for cover when they saw that armed hand grenade in the boy's trembling hand, no one got hurt. As they gritted their teeth waiting for the explosion, all they heard was silence . . .

. . . then Stump's wailing voice, "I can't do anything right!"

Like the other grenades that had been packed in the black bag I hid in the dumpster, the one that Stump had been carrying around with him turned out to be a dud. The only way his father could bring back hand grenades as sou-venirs from his tour of duty was if they'd been disarmed—although that hadn't kept Mr. Teeter from bragging about his collection of "live" grenades.

Stump might still be tried as an adult for shooting his

father and "attempting a terrorist act," but the rumor around school is that he's not going to be sentenced to a juvie detention facility like Grey Cook. Jackson Teeter is probably headed for a psychiatric treatment center.

Another reason my face vanished so fast from the news shows probably was my usual unexciting reply whenever a reporter asked me how I felt about what I'd done.

"What I did was nothing," I said.

They didn't understand that. The only part they liked was one answer I gave to CNN: "If I did do anything worthwhile it's because of my uncle, who's been teaching me about The Way."

I was sorry as soon as I said that. They tried to spin it that I'd been training to be a ninja or some kind of superhero.

I got a little teasing at school when I went back, but it was friendly. Some kids actually came up to me and shook my hand and said things like they hoped I was healing up okay and they thought I was cool. (Maya among them. Which truly is cool.)

But now it's like nothing happened. True, I do get a nod from the A.P. whenever he sees me in the hall, but that's about it. Nobody pays any special attention to me anymore. Which is okay by me. I've learned that being anonymous is not bad at all.

What's sad is that most of the kids at Long River High just act as if the whole incident never happened. Same cliques, same music, same stuff, different day. The school has started a new program to counteract bullying, but who knows how much that can really change things? I can only hope.

Dad called from the West Coast while I was in the hospital. He'd gotten the message from Mom on his answering service at about the same time he saw me being interviewed on FOX.

"Are you okay, son?" I knew he was asking me much more than that.

"I'm okay, Dad. I really am."

"I'll be back East in a week. I know we have a lot to talk about. I'm so sorry, Cody."

What little hope I might have had that my parents were going to get back together left me then. But so did some of the pain I'd been feeling about my family being torn apart. My mom was still my mom. My dad would always be my father, even if the two of them weren't able to live together. I didn't understand why things were that way. I didn't like it. But I knew that if I had to, I could accept it.

"It's okay, Dad," I said. I was crying by then, and I could hear that he was crying, too, at the other end of the line.

"This summer," he said, "we'll take a week and go camping together. I promise."

"I know we will," I said. And I meant it just as much as he did. We were telling each other the truth.

We kept talking for a while after that. Because of all the medicine they were pumping into me, I don't remember much of the rest of our conversation, aside from his saying two or three times that he was really looking forward to meeting Uncle John. And the words he spoke just before we hung up.

"I'm so proud of you, son."

So I guess some good did come out of it.

Plus my being on TV did focus some attention on Uncle John, and even though he didn't particularly care for it, the organizers of the War at the Shore saw it as great publicity for them. They conveniently forgot that they'd refused him entry when he first applied and only grudgingly let him in because of my mom's influence. Even though they figured him for a "fish," an inexperienced guy the others would eat up, they played up his being part of the tournament.

But after his first win, and then his second, they realized that what they'd let loose wasn't just a fish, but a shark.

The coolest part for me was the way Uncle John won each of his matches. In a mixed-martial-arts fight with six-ounce gloves, some fighters prefer to do their work as strikers, throwing blow after blow and kick after kick from a standing position or by getting on top of their opponent and going to what they call "ground and pound."

Uncle John, though, won each of his first three fights with as little violence and as much finesse as possible, ducking, blocking, pulling guard, and then putting his opponents into Gracie ju-jitsu holds that have led to their submitting by tapping out. A triangle choke in match number one, a flying guillotine in the second, a kimura wrist lock that quickly transitioned into an arm bar in the third. Fighting without fighting.

This last bout, though, is supposed to be his toughest. This opponent looks twice as big as my uncle. He's been a UFC fighter for four years and was a finalist in the *Ultimate Fighter* TV show.

The referee starts the fight. They tap gloves. The other guy has seen Uncle John's last two fights and is determined not to let it go to the ground. As soon as they've tapped gloves, the other guy does a lightning-fast spinning backfist.

But to me it looks like he's moving in slow motion. And I know it's that way for my uncle, too, as he ducks under that fist and leaps like a panther onto his opponent's back, pulling him down to the canvas. He has an arm locked around the guy's neck. It's a textbook rear naked choke.

And it's over. The guy has tapped. Uncle John wins. He is helping his former adversary to his feet, and the two of them are hugging and shaking hands. Even though the other fighter lost, he's smiling in admiration at Uncle John's technique. It's the kind of sportsmanship that has made my uncle love this fight game so much.

There's stunned silence from the crowd. It all happened so fast that most of the people didn't even see it. Then the twenty-second-long match starts to be replayed again and again on the big screens around the octagon. The referee raises Uncle John's hand, and people finally start cheering and applauding.

Uncle John makes that gesture again. Two fingers raised to the sky in a circle before bringing them back to touch his heart and then thrust forward. Indian sign language silently speaking an old wisdom from the heart of all creation.

My left arm is still in a sling, so Mom helps me climb up on the ring apron where Uncle John is now pressing the palm of his hand against the mesh of the cage. I put my palm against his.

"We did it, Cody!" he says, leaning his head close. "Remember our deal? Fifty-fifty on my winnings. You and your mother are going to get a new car and move out of that ratty trailer!"

I grin back at him. Then, as Mom holds me up from behind, I raise my own hand in that same gesture my uncle made.

All power comes from our Creator.

All things are connected.

There is peace within me as I follow The Way.

The straight branch
may be bent into a hoop.
—Pendetta Satu

About the Author

With more than 120 books and numerous awards to his credit, **Joseph Bruchac** is best known for his work as a Native writer and storyteller. However, he was also a varsity heavyweight wrestler at Cornell University and is a former high school and junior high wrestling coach. And, for more than three decades, he has also been a devoted student of the martial arts.

He holds the ranks of pengawal and pendekar in pencak-silat, the martial art of Indonesia, and has studied various forms of tai chi, capoeira, kung fu wu su, and Brazilian jiu-jitsu with numerous teachers. He does not regard himself as a master.

His two sons—and frequent collaborators in writing and story-telling—Jim and Jesse, are also martial arts teachers. Jim is a sensei and fourth degree black belt in karate, and Jesse is co-owner of a mixed martial arts academy. (See www.wnymma.com)

Mr. Bruchac lives in Greenfield Center, New York, with Carol, his wife of 42 years, whose oft-repeated mantra to her slightly crazed husband and sons has been: "Please try not to get hurt too much."

Olakamigenoka
Make Peace